Red Clay Redemption

The Toby Siler Story

CHARLES E. CRAVEY

IN HIS STEPS PUBLISHING

ISBN: 978-1-58535-124-4 (Paper)

ISBN: 978-1-58535-125-1 (Kindle)

Library of Congress Catalog Number: 2025910942

Published by In His Steps Publishing Company, Statesboro, Georgia, USA

Contents

Introduction

At the age of twenty, I was honored to become Georgia's first COM-MUNITY WORKER for the Department of Juvenile Justice. For three years, I served in this capacity, working closely with both male and female offenders in the system. My role entrusted me with the responsibility of representing them in court, advising judges on sentencing, and advocating for their futures. It was during this pivotal time that I received a calling to full-time ministry in The United Methodist Church—an incredible journey that would shape the next fifty years of my life.

My path to this work was unconventional. As a seventh grader, I found myself in trouble, placed on probation, and watched over by an officer who saw potential in me. Years later, he offered me the role of community worker, believing I had shown remarkable growth during his tenure. That trust gave me purpose, and I carried it forward—transporting runaways back to Georgia, accompanying young people to Youth Development Centers, and bringing them home once they had served their time.

Over the decades, I have witnessed immense hardship, listened to the stories of struggling juveniles, and stood beside them in their pain. My heart still beats for them and their brokenness, and I pray daily that each one will find a path to healing and new life.

It is up to all of us to offer guidance, hope, and opportunity to the youth of today—so they may step into a better tomorrow. The journey begins with us.

The Rev. Dr. Charles E. Cravey
June 2025

1

Roots in Red Clay

———◆◇◆———

P itney wasn't much to look at from the outside—just a modest town nestled in the red clay hills of middle Georgia. A handful of streets, a single textile factory, and a smattering of farms made up most of what there was to see. But for the 3,000 or so people who called it home, Pitney was more than a place on the map. It was a community where time seemed to stretch a little longer and everyone's business was everyone's business.

Our house sat on the edge of town; a simple clapboard dwelling perched on a clay hill surrounded by sprawling fields. Life was plain but steady, built on the rhythms of farm chores, Mama's endless baking, and the hum of the factory whistle echoing through the air.

Mama—Madie Lee Compton Siler—was the heart of our family. Her hands were never idle, whether she was sewing patches onto my worn trousers, kneading dough for her famous pecan pies, or calming the occasional storm that rose between Daddy and Robbie. Her voice carried a quiet strength, and her faith in us—especially in me—was unshakable, even when I gave her reasons to worry.

Daddy was a different story. Carl Siler was a farmer and a World War II Marine veteran, a man hardened by years of labor and the memories of battles fought at Midway and Iwo Jima. Though he stood a head shorter than most men, his presence loomed large in any room. He was a man of few words, and the ones he did speak often carried the weight of expectation.

When he was sober, Daddy's discipline was strict but fair. But on the nights when whiskey dulled the lines between his wartime past and his present life, his temper could boil over, leaving us to tiptoe around the jagged edges of his mood. Robbie withstood the worst of it more often than I did, a quiet protector who shielded me from the worst of Daddy's wrath.

Robbie, four years my senior, worked hard on the farm with Daddy. He was strong and agile and was everything I aspired to be—strong, confident, and endlessly patient. If Daddy's approval was a moving target, Robbie seemed to hit the mark more often than not.

When life on the farm felt too heavy, I found escape in the company of my two best friends, Larry and Carl. Carl Jenkins—a wiry, freckled boy from a small community called Sinkhole, just down the dirt road from our home.

Larry, the ringleader of our trio, was fearless to the point of recklessness. With his wild red hair and boundless energy, he seemed to thrive on the thrill of daring adventures. He could climb the tallest tree or chase down hogs in the field with the kind of confidence that left Carl and me shaking our heads in awe.

Sinkhole Creek was our playground, a winding ribbon of water that ran through the countryside and offered endless opportunities for exploration. We spent our days fishing for bream, catfish, and pike, our nights lit by the soft glow of the moon as we hunted bullfrogs along the banks. Mama's fried bullfrog legs, served with a side of buttery grits, were our hard-earned prize after those nighttime escapades.

The creek wasn't just a place; it was a world unto itself. There was a spot called the Bull Hole—a deep, mysterious pool said to have no bottom. Though I never believed the old tales, I'll never forget the night I nearly drowned there, only to be saved by Larry's quick thinking and stronger-than-you'd-think arms. That moment sealed a bond between us that not even time could erode.

Just down the dirt road from our farm lived the Rucker family, one of the few Black families in Pitney. Their modest home sat beneath the protective shade of an old oak tree, its sprawling branches spreading wide like open arms. Billy Rucker, their youngest, was my age, and despite the quiet lines of segregation that marked the South in those days, he was one of my closest friends.

Billy and I were bound by a shared love for baseball. On warm summer evenings, we'd meet at the edge of the dirt road, gloves in hand, ready to toss a ball back and forth until the fireflies came out. His laughter was contagious, his smile bright enough to outshine the prejudices of a world that often seemed intent on keeping us apart.

"You ever think about playing for Pitney High?" He asked once, his voice light but his eyes serious.

I shrugged, adjusting the laces on my glove. "I'd like to, but I'm pretty sure Coach Miller's got his eye on somebody else."

Billy laughed, tossing the ball back to me. "Well, when you make the team, don't forget about me. Maybe I'll be in the stands one day, cheering you on."

His words stayed with me, though they carried an unspoken truth—that for all his talent, Billy would never have the same chances I did. It wasn't fair, but fairness wasn't something Pitney promised to anyone, least of all someone like Billy.

For all the joy I found in my friendships, there was a magnetic pull toward mischief that I couldn't seem to resist. Larry's fearless nature often led us into trouble, like the time we snuck into the old feed mill after dark, daring each other to climb the rafters.

"Bet you can't make it to the top," Larry taunted, his grin wide as he scrambled up the wooden beams.

"Oh yeah?" I shot back, the thrill of the challenge outweighing any thought of consequence.

By the time the town sheriff showed up the next morning, word had already spread that "those Siler boys and their friends" had been up to no good again. Daddy's face was like stone as he listened to the sheriff's warning, his silence more unnerving than any outburst could have been. That night, his belt left welts on my back that stung long after the lesson was over.

But even then, the pull of rebellion wasn't something I could shake. It wasn't that I wanted to defy Daddy or embarrass Mama; it was that the boundaries of our small-town life felt too tight, too confining.

I wanted more—more freedom, more adventure, more of whatever waited beyond Pitney's borders.

2

A Day Too Far

———◆◇◆———

It started like any other humid summer morning in Pitney. The air was thick and heavy, clinging to my skin as I sat on the porch sipping iced tea. Mama's voice floated out from the kitchen, where she was busy preparing supper for later that evening. The sweet, familiar smell of her pecan pies already wafted through the open window.

"Toby!" her voice called, carrying the strength of someone used to her boys being just out of reach. "You best get a move on before your daddy starts hollering."

"Yes, ma'am!" I yelled back, slipping on my boots.

Out in the field, Daddy was already at work, his weathered hands moving with a precision born of decades of farming. His posture was as rigid as the fence he was repairing, and his hat shaded the sharp angles of his face. Robbie was nearby, whistling to himself as he loaded bales of hay onto the truck bed.

"'Bout time, boy," Daddy grunted when he saw me approaching. He handed me a pair of pliers without another word, and I took my place beside him.

We worked silently for a while, the sound of the wind rustling through the trees the only company. Robbie's occasional quips about the heat or the stubbornness of the hogs lightened the mood, but Daddy was laser focused.

"Keep it tight," Daddy said as I worked the wire into place. "You don't want another break." "Yes, sir," I replied, though my hands fumbled slightly under his watchful eye.

Robbie caught the slip and leaned over with a grin. "Relax, Tob. The fence ain't gonna fight back."

I smiled despite myself, but the tension in Daddy's presence never fully left.

It was mid-afternoon when Larry and Carl showed up, their shirts dusty and their expressions full of mischief. I caught sight of them from across the yard, standing just off the porch and waving me over like conspirators with a secret.

"Toby!" Larry called, his voice barely above a whisper, but his tone practically dripping with excitement.

I hesitated, glancing toward Daddy, who was focused on the next section of fence. Robbie was retying the tarp on the truck bed; his movements deliberate as he pretended not to notice.

"You'd best think really hard about this," Robbie said under his breath, his eyes not leaving the tarp. "Daddy won't take kindly to you wandering off."

He was right, of course, but curiosity—or maybe something closer to desperation—got the better of me. With a hasty promise to be back soon, I set down the pliers and jogged over to meet Larry and Carl.

"You're not gonna believe what we've got lined up," Larry said, his grin wide and reckless.

"You remember those houses on the edge of town?" Carl added, glancing over his shoulder as if the sheriff himself might appear any second.

I nodded, unease already starting to creep in.

"They're empty during the day," Larry continued. "Their folks all work at the factory, so we figured, why not? Just a quick in-and-out, grab a little something, and no one's the wiser."

I swallowed hard, the weight of what they were suggesting settling in my chest. "I don't know, guys. I've got a lot to do here, and if my daddy finds out—"

"He won't," Larry interrupted, his confidence infectious. "C'mon, Tob. It'll be just like old times."

Carl nodded, his nervous grin betraying his own doubts. "What's the harm? We're not taking anything big—just some pocket change and knickknacks."

Against my better judgment, I agreed. Maybe it was the pull of adventure, the need to escape the shadow of Daddy's expectations, or just the desire to belong. Either way, I found myself following them down the dusty road toward town, my heart pounding with both fear and excitement.

The first house was easy—too easy. Larry had a knack for spotting weaknesses, and within minutes, we were inside, pocketing loose change and small trinkets. Carl kept watch by the window, his freckled face pale but determined.

The second house was much the same, and by the time we reached the third, my nerves had started to settle. This was just another harmless escapade, I told myself, nothing that would cause real harm.

But as I rifled through a drawer in the living room, the sound of a door creaking open shattered the illusion.

"Someone's here!" Carl hissed from his post near the back door, his voice barely audible over the pounding of my own heartbeat.

"Stay calm," Larry whispered, though his eyes darted nervously around the room.

Before we could react, a man's voice rang out, sharp and commanding. "Who's there?"

The next few seconds blurred into a frantic rush of movement. We scrambled toward the back door, our stolen goods forgotten in the chaos. My foot caught on the edge of the carpet, sending me sprawling onto the floor. Larry grabbed my arm, hauling me up as the man's footsteps drew closer.

"Let's go!" he shouted, pulling me out the door and into the yard.

We ran until my lungs burned and my legs threatened to give out, disappearing into the thick woods that bordered the edge of town.

By the time we emerged from the woods, our panic had been replaced by a shaky kind of relief. We laughed nervously, brushing off the dirt and leaves that clung to our clothes.

"See?" Larry said, his grin returning. "Piece of cake."

But our relief was short-lived. As we approached Main Street, the sheriff's patrol car came into view, parked in front of the diner. Sheriff Green stepped out, his expression grim and his posture straight as an arrow.

"Boys," he said, his voice heavy with disappointment. "We need to have a word."

The ride to the station felt like an eternity, the air thick with unspoken dread. By the time we arrived, the reality of what we'd done had fully sunk in.

"You're lucky no one got hurt," Sheriff Green said as we sat in his office, our heads bowed like scolded children. "But luck only goes so far. You're gonna have to answer for this."

Sheriff Green made us empty all our pockets, and he discovered the coins we had stolen and a few dollar bills. We had been "caught," and now there was nothing we could do about it.

When Mama and Daddy arrived at the station, the look on Mama's face nearly broke me. Her eyes were red, her hands clutching her purse so tightly her knuckles were white. Daddy's expression was harder to read, but his silence spoke volumes.

"We'll deal with him," Daddy said to the sheriff, his voice low but steady.

Mama didn't say a word as we walked out to the car. It wasn't until we were halfway home that she finally turned to me, her voice trembling. "Toby, how could you?"

"I'm sorry, Mama," I whispered, my throat tight.

"Sorry doesn't fix it," Daddy said, his eyes fixed on the road ahead. "You've brought shame to this family, boy."

The courthouse in Pitney was a modest building, its whitewashed walls, and creaky wooden floors a far cry from the grandeur you'd see in the movies. But to me, it felt like the most intimidating place in the world.

The judge, a stern white-haired man with sharp eyes and a voice that carried authority, addressed us after hearing the evidence.

"Toby Siler," he said finally, "you've made a grave error in judgment. But I believe there's still hope for you."

He sentenced me to one year at the Macon Industrial Home for Boys—a decision that felt both merciful and devastating. The sound of the gavel striking the bench was final, a punctuation mark on the chapter of my life I had just closed.

3

The Walls That Hold You

The Macon Industrial Home for Boys stood on the outskirts of town, a gray, imposing structure surrounded by acres of empty land. The ride there was eerily silent, broken only by the faint hum of Reverend Tanner's old car as it rumbled over cracked pavement. Reverend Tanner, the local Methodist minister and my court-appointed chaperone, had been assigned to escort me. Though he wasn't unkind, he had the air of a man who didn't shy away from uncomfortable truths.

As the home came into view, I felt my stomach churn. Its high fences, topped with rusted barbed wire, loomed like a physical embodiment of the shame I carried. A guard stood at the gate; his expression set in stone as Reverend Tanner pulled to a stop.

"This is where we part ways," Reverend Tanner said, his tone even. "You've got a hard road ahead, Toby, but it doesn't have to be the end of the line. Remember that."

I nodded mutely, stepping out of the car and gripping my small duffel bag tightly. As the gate creaked open, the sound seemed to echo in my chest, each step toward the entrance feeling heavier than the last. I was escorted by the guard into the recesses of this foreboding place.

Inside, the air was thick with the mingled scents of sweat and disinfectant. A man who introduced himself as Mr. Reed, one of the senior staff members, guided me through the intake process. His voice was brisk, his manner efficient, as he rattled off a list of rules and expectations.

"No fighting. No talking back. And absolutely no escaping," he said, his eyes narrowing as he handed me a neatly folded uniform. "You do your time, and you do it right. Understood?"

"Yes, sir," I mumbled, feeling smaller than I ever had before.

The boys were lined up in the cafeteria when I was introduced to the group. Mr. Reed clapped his hands, and the low buzz of conversation died down immediately.

"This is Siler," he announced, his tone brooking no argument. "You'll treat him like you treat any other boy here—with respect."

I scanned the crowd, meeting wary stares and sizing glances from boys of all shapes and sizes. Some looked curious, others indifferent, but a few—like the hulking figure in the corner who smirked when our eyes met—made my pulse quicken with unease.

The days that followed were grueling. Mornings began with the shrill blare of an alarm, dragging us out of bed before the sun had fully risen. Breakfast was a hurried affair—oatmeal, toast, and weak coffee served in silence—before we were marched off to our assigned duties.

For me, that meant hours in the industrial shop, learning the ins and outs of carpentry. At first, the work felt monotonous, the scent of sawdust and oil thick in the air as I fumbled with tools I barely knew how to use. But there was something oddly grounding about it, a rhythm that allowed me to lose myself in the task and momentarily forget the weight of my circumstances. After our work, we spent several hours in a classroom learning.

Not everyone was as willing to keep their head down. Darryl Haney, a wiry boy with a sharp tongue and a penchant for trouble, quickly established himself as the alpha of our dormitory. His sidekick, Pete Sutton, was a wall of muscle with a mean streak that left me constantly glancing over my shoulder.

"What's your deal, new kid?" Darryl asked one evening as we cleaned up after dinner. His tone was mocking, but his eyes were calculating.

"Just trying to get through my time," I replied carefully, keeping my gaze steady despite the unease curling in my gut.

Darryl smirked. "We'll see about that."

Not everyone at the home was looking for a fight. Ziggy, a quiet boy with a mop of curly hair and a talent for blending into the background, became my first friend.

"You'll get used to it," he said one night as we lay in our bunks, the soft hum of the overhead lights filling the silence. "The routine, the rules... it gets easier." "Does it?" I asked skeptically, turning to face him.

He shrugged. "Easier doesn't mean better. But you make do."

Ziggy's calm demeanor was a balm in an environment that often felt like a powder keg waiting to explode. We stuck together during meals and assignments, finding moments of levity in a place that seemed determined to crush any trace of hope.

It didn't take long for trouble to find me. During an afternoon in the industrial shop, Pete Sutton cornered me as I was sanding down a wooden plank.

"You think you're better than us, don't you?" He said, his voice low but menacing.

I shook my head, keeping my eyes on the plank. "I'm just doing my work."

Pete leaned closer, his breath hot against my ear. "That's not how it works around here, new kid. You've got to earn your place."

Before I could respond, Mr. Rogers, one of the instructors, appeared out of nowhere. "Sutton," he barked, his tone sharp. "You've got your own work to do. Leave Siler alone."

Pete glared at me but backed off, muttering under his breath.

Mr. Rogers turned to me, his expression stern but not unkind. "You alright?"

"Yes, sir," I replied, my voice steadier than I felt.

He nodded. "Good. Keep your head down and focus on your work. Let me handle the rest."

That night, as I lay in bed staring at the cracked ceiling, I replayed the events of the day in my mind. For all the challenges, there were moments—small, fleeting moments—that hinted at the possibility of something better.

Mr. Rogers' intervention, Ziggy's quiet friendship, the rhythm of the carpentry shop—it wasn't much, but it was enough to keep me going.

As I closed my eyes, I made a silent promise to myself: I would survive this. No matter how hard it got, no matter how heavy the weight of my mistakes, I would find a way through.

4

Foundations of Change

The days at the Macon Industrial Home fell into a rhythm that was as relentless as it was numbing. Each morning began the same way—the harsh blare of the alarm jolting us awake before dawn, followed by a hurried march to the cafeteria for a breakfast that rarely deviated from oatmeal, toast, and watery coffee. After that, we were assigned to our daily duties, which for me meant hours in the industrial shop.

At first, the work felt meaningless, a way to keep us busy while we served out our sentences. But as the days turned to weeks, I began to find a strange kind of solace in the steady hum of the machinery, the scent of sawdust thick in the air. There was something satisfying about watching a rough piece of wood transform under my hands, each precise cut and careful sanding bringing it closer to its final form. It was, in its own way, a reminder that things— people—could change with enough time and effort.

My time in the industrial shop was supervised by Mr. Rogers, a no-nonsense instructor with graying hair and a sharp eye for detail. He rarely raised his voice, but there was an authority in his presence that made you sit up straighter when he walked into the room.

"You're rough with the tools, Siler," he said one afternoon, watching as I struggled to cut a plank of wood evenly. "You can't force it. Let the saw do the work."

I sighed, setting the saw down. "I'm trying."

"No, you're not," he replied, his tone blunt but not unkind. "You're fighting it. That's your problem—you think you have to muscle your way through everything."

His words stung, but they stuck with me. Over the next few weeks, I began to approach my work differently, focusing less on brute strength and more on precision and patience. It wasn't just about the tools—it was about me, about learning to control the storm that had been building inside me for as long as I could remember.

Life in the dormitory was a different kind of challenge. With close to thirty boys crammed into a space designed for half that number, tensions often ran high. Arguments over bunk space, stolen food, or even a sideways glance were common, and fights could erupt with little warning.

Darryl Haney and Pete Sutton were at the center of most of the trouble, their dominance over the dorm enforced through a combination of intimidation and brute force. I did my best to avoid them, but they seemed to have a knack for sniffing out weakness, and they were relentless in their pursuit of control.

"You think you're better than us, Siler?" Darryl sneered one evening, cornering me in the hallway as Pete loomed behind him. "You think because you can keep your head down, we'll let you off easy?"

I kept my voice steady, though my hands clenched into fists at my sides. "I'm just here to do my time, same as you."

Darryl laughed, a low, menacing sound. "We'll see about that."

Amid the chaos of the dormitory, Ziggy remained a constant source of quiet strength. He had a way of diffusing tension with a well-timed joke or a calm word, and his ability to stay out of the crosshairs was something I admired deeply.

"Don't let them get to you," he said one night as we sat on the edge of our bunks, the sounds of the dorm settling into a restless quiet around us. "They bark more than they bite."

"Easy for you to say," I muttered. "They don't come after you."

Ziggy smiled faintly. "That's because I don't give them a reason to. You've got to pick your battles, Toby. Sometimes, the best way to win is not to play."

It was advice that stuck with me, though I didn't fully understand it at the time. Ziggy's ability to navigate the harsh realities of the Industrial Home with quiet resilience was something I began to aspire to, even as I struggled to find my own path.

About a month into my sentence, I had my first real taste of respect—not from Mr. Rogers or the staff, but from the boys themselves. It happened during a rare afternoon of free time, when a group of us had gathered in the yard for a makeshift game of basketball.

Darryl and Pete had claimed one side of the court, their dominance over the game mirroring their control of the dorm. Ziggy and I, along with a few others who were tired of being pushed around, decided it was time to challenge them.

The game was rough, elbows flying, insults hurled, the ball slipping from sweaty hands as we fought for every point. Darryl's temper flared when we took the lead, and I found myself on the receiving end of a shove that sent me sprawling into the dirt.

"Stay down, Siler," he spat, his eyes blazing.

But I didn't. I stood, wiping the blood from my lip and meeting his glare head-on. "Not a chance."

The game ended in a narrow victory for our side, and while Darryl and Pete retreated with muttered threats, the other boys clapped me on the back, their smiles wide and genuine.

"You've got guts, Siler," Ziggy said, his tone carrying a note of approval I hadn't realized I was craving.

That night, as I lay in bed staring at the cracked ceiling, I thought about the lessons I'd learned so far—not just from the basketball game, but from every moment I'd spent in the Industrial Home. Mr. Rogers' advice about control, Ziggy's quiet wisdom, the camaraderie I'd begun to build with the other boys—all of it was shaping me, piece by piece.

For the first time, I began to see my time at the home not as a punishment but as an opportunity. It wasn't about surviving anymore—it was about becoming someone better.

And for the first time, I thought just maybe I could.

5

A Year in the Shadows

The seasons changed with barely a whisper within the confines of the Industrial Home, marked only by the slow creeping of frost on the windows or the sweltering heat that hung heavy in the dorms. Life inside was a world unto itself—a relentless routine that blurred the days together but also provided an unexpected sense of structure.

By now, I had carved out a small place for myself in this strange, harsh environment. I wasn't the new kid anymore, but I wasn't anyone important either, and I was content to keep it that way. The lessons I'd learned from Ziggy—about staying under the radar and picking my battles—had served me well, though there were still moments when trouble found me despite my best efforts.

It happened one muggy afternoon in the yard, the kind of day where the heat pressed down on you like a weight. A group of us had gathered for a pick-up basketball game, the court's cracked asphalt shimmering in the sun.

Darryl Haney, as always, was at the center of the action, his voice loud and his elbows sharper than necessary. Pete Sutton loomed nearby, ready to back him up at a moment's notice.

"C'mon, Siler," Darryl called, his smirk laced with challenge. "Think you can keep up?"

I hesitated, glancing at Ziggy, who shook his head slightly. But something in me—a mix of pride and frustration—made me step onto the court.

The game was brutal. Darryl played dirty, shoving and tripping without hesitation, and I found myself gritting my teeth as the tension between us escalated. When I managed to steal the ball and sink a shot over him, his temper boiled over.

"You think you're hot stuff, huh?" He spat, shoving me hard enough to send me stumbling back.

I straightened, meeting his glare with a calmness I didn't entirely feel. "Just playing the game, Haney. You ought to try it sometime."

The other boys laughed, and for a moment, I thought I'd won. But Darryl's scowl deepened, and I braced myself for the fight I was sure was coming.

Before he could make a move, Mr. Rogers appeared, his presence like a bucket of cold water on the rising tension.

"Break it up," he said firmly, his eyes sharp. "Haney, you're benched. Siler, keep your head in the game."

Darryl stalked off, muttering curses under his breath, and I let out a quiet breath of relief.

"You handled that well," Ziggy said later, his tone carrying a note of approval. "He'll push you again, but you didn't let him win this time."

One of the most unexpected challenges came during night watch duty, a rotating responsibility that every boy in the dorm had to take on at some point. It wasn't much—a few hours spent patrolling the hallways to make sure everything was in order—but the quiet, lonely stretches of time often brought with them a flood of thoughts I wasn't ready to face.

One particular night, as I paced the dimly lit corridors, I found myself thinking about Pitney. I thought of Mama's pecan pies, of Daddy's stern voice, and of Robbie's easy grin. I wondered if they thought of me too, if they were still angry, or if they missed me even a little. And then, there was Laura. I had met her in the fourth grade, and she took my heart in an instant. It was like we were destined to be together, but now we were apart, and I had wondered if she still liked me after my trouble.

The sound of footsteps broke through my reverie, and I turned to see Mr. Rogers approaching.

"Couldn't sleep either?" he asked, his voice low but kind.

I shrugged, leaning against the wall. "Just doing my shift."

He nodded, studying me for a moment before speaking again. "You've been doing better, Siler.

Keeping your head down, staying out of trouble. That's good."

"Trying to," I replied, though my voice carried a note of uncertainty.

Mr. Rogers tilted his head slightly, his expression thoughtful. "You know, it's not just about staying out of trouble. It's about figuring out who you want to be—what kind of man you want to become. Have you thought about that?"

I hesitated, the weight of his question pressing down on me. "I guess I haven't figured that out yet."

He smiled faintly. "That's okay. Figuring it out is part of the process. Just don't forget—who you were doesn't have to define who you'll be."

His words stayed with me long after he'd walked away, echoing in the quiet of the dorm as I returned to my patrol.

Toward the end of my first six months, I experienced my first real taste of success. The industrial shop was hosting a woodworking competition—a chance for the boys to display their skills and earn a few small privileges, like extra recreation time or a slightly better meal.

I poured everything I had into my project—a simple but carefully crafted wooden chair. The process was painstaking, each cut and joint a test of my patience and precision. But when I finally sanded down the last rough edge and polished the wood to a warm shine, I felt a sense of pride I hadn't known in a long time.

When the results were announced and my name was called, the applause from my peers felt like a balm, a reminder that even here, in this harsh and unforgiving place, I could still accomplish something.

Mr. Rogers clapped me on the back, his grin wide. "Told you that you had it in you, Siler." For the first time, I believed him.

6

The End of a Long Road

———◆◇◆———

The days at the Macon Industrial Home blurred together as my sentence neared its end. What had once seemed impossible—a year in this place—was now something I could look back on with a mix of exhaustion and quiet pride. I had survived the harsh realities of the home, the strict rules, the tense dormitory dynamics, and the grueling hours in the industrial shop. More than that, I had changed—though I wasn't yet sure how deep or lasting that change would be.

By now, even Darryl Haney and Pete Sutton had stopped bothering me. Ziggy said it was because I'd earned their respect—through basketball games, through my work in the shop, and through refusing to back down even when things got tough. I wasn't sure I'd call it respect, but the quiet was something I didn't take for granted.

On one of my last afternoons in the industrial shop, Mr. Rogers pulled me aside.

"You've done good work here, Siler," he said, his voice steady as he inspected the wooden chest I'd just finished. "More than good, really."

I smiled faintly, wiping my hands on the worn rag in my pocket. "Thanks, Mr. Rogers. It means a lot."

He nodded, his expression thoughtful. "But you know, this isn't just about woodworking. The skills you've learned here—they're about more than building furniture. They're about building yourself. Do you get what I'm saying?"

I hesitated, the weight of his words settling over me. "I think so."

He smiled then, a rare, genuine smile that felt like a small gift. "Good. Because that's what I want you to take with you when you leave. Remember—it's not just about what you can do with your hands. It's about what you can do with your heart and your head, too."

The last week at the Industrial Home was bittersweet. On one hand, I was eager—desperate, even—to leave and return to Pitney, to my family, to the life I'd left behind. But on the other hand, there was a sense of loss that I couldn't quite name.

Ziggy, who had become my closest friend here, was one of the hardest goodbyes.

"You're gonna do great out there, Toby," he said, his tone light but sincere as we sat together in the dorm on my final night.

"Thanks, Zig," I replied, my throat tight. "I don't think I'd have made it through this without you."

He smiled, brushing off the compliment with a wave of his hand. "Ah, you'd have been fine.

But... I'm glad we stuck together anyway."

The other boys offered their own farewells in their own ways—a nod here, a slap on the back there. Even Darryl managed a gruff "Take care," which felt more like a victory than anything else.

Before I left, Mr. Rogers called me into his office.

"You've got potential, Toby," he said, his voice steady as he leaned back in his chair. "I've seen it in the way you've carried yourself here, the way you've worked, and the way you've handled challenges. Don't let that potential go to waste."

"I won't," I promised, the words carrying a weight that felt both comforting and daunting.

He nodded; his expression serious. "Good. Because you've got a chance to turn your life around now—a real chance. And I hope you take it."

The morning of my release was crisp and quiet, the early sunlight spilling over the gray walls of the Industrial Home. As I walked toward the gates with my duffel bag slung over my shoulder, the sound of the creaking metal felt like the first breath of freedom I'd taken in a year.

Reverend Tanner was waiting for me on the other side, his expression calm but approving.

"Welcome back to the world, Toby," he said as I climbed into his car. "Are you ready for the next step?"

I nodded, though the truth was, I wasn't entirely sure. But as the car pulled away from the home and the gates disappeared into the distance, I felt something stir within me—a spark of hope, of possibility.

I didn't know exactly what the future held, but I knew one thing for certain: I was ready to face it.

7

Crossing the Divide

———◆◇◆———

The dirt road leading home felt longer than I remembered, the familiar bends and curves stretching endlessly as Reverend Tanner's car bounced along. Each mile brought a new wave of anticipation and unease. I had spent the last year imagining this moment—wondering what it would feel like to step back onto the clay hill, to face Mama and Daddy, and to see Pitney with fresh eyes. Now that it was here, I wasn't sure I was ready.

Reverend Tanner glanced at me as we rounded the final curve, his expression thoughtful. "You've got a good family waiting for you, Toby. That's more than some boys can say. But don't expect everything to be the same as it was."

"I know," I replied, my voice quiet.

He nodded. "Take it one step at a time. Give them reason to believe in you again."

As the house came into view, my heart quickened. The familiar porch, the weathered shingles, the swing where Robbie and I had spent countless afternoons—it was all the same, yet it felt different. Smaller, somehow.

Mama was on the porch, her hands clasped tightly in front of her. The moment the car stopped, she hurried down the steps, pulling me into a hug before I could say a word.

"Oh, Toby," she whispered, her voice thick with emotion. "It's so good to have you home."

I held on to her, my chest tightening with a mix of relief and guilt. "I'm sorry, Mama," I murmured.

She pulled back slightly, brushing a strand of hair from my face. "We'll talk about all that later. Right now, I'm just glad you're here."

Daddy was waiting on the porch, his arms crossed and his expression unreadable. When I approached, he gave a small nod, but his eyes searched mine as if looking for something he wasn't sure he'd find.

"Welcome back," he said simply, extending a hand.

I took it, the grip firm and brief. "Thank you, sir."

For a moment, we stood in silence, the weight of unspoken words hanging heavy between us. Finally, he turned and headed back into the house, his footsteps steady and deliberate.

"It'll take time," Mama said quietly, placing a hand on my arm. "He's glad you're home, even if he doesn't say it."

The house smelled like biscuits and fried chicken, a comforting reminder of the life I'd left behind. Robbie was sitting at the kitchen table, his face lighting up when he saw me.

"'Bout time," he said with a grin, pulling me into a bear hug.

"It's good to see you, Rob," I replied, my voice thick with emotion.

We sat together, talking quietly about the year that had passed. Robbie filled me in on the latest news around town—the neighbors who'd moved away, the new family that had taken over the grocery store, and the championship win for Pitney High's baseball team.

But beneath the surface of our conversation, there was an undercurrent of caution, a recognition that things had changed.

Reverend Tanner was not a man of idle words. He had a way of speaking that carried both authority and compassion, making every sentence feel like both a challenge and a gift. Our meetings quickly became more than just routine check-ins—they were moments of reflection, where he gently pushed me to confront myself in ways I hadn't dared to before.

One afternoon, as we sat in his office at the Methodist church, the light filtering through the stained-glass windows cast colorful patterns on the worn carpet. Reverend Tanner leaned back in his chair, his Bible resting open on the desk beside him.

"You're doing well, Toby," he said, his tone even but warm. "Your family's starting to see it. The community's watching. But the real question is, do you see it?"

I hesitated, the weight of his words pressing down on me. "I don't know. I'm trying to be better, but... sometimes it feels like it's not enough."

He nodded, his expression thoughtful. "That's the thing about change. It's slow, and it's hard, and sometimes it feels like you're not moving at all. But every day you choose to do the right thing—that's a step forward. And those steps add up."

I looked down at my hands, the calluses from the Industrial Home still rough against my skin. "It's just... hard to get past what people think of me. Like, no matter what I do, it'll always be there."

Reverend Tanner leaned forward, his voice soft but firm. "People's opinions aren't what defines you, Toby. It's your actions, your choices. Every day, you have a chance to show them who you are—not who you were. But you've got to believe it first."

His words lingered with me as I left the church that afternoon, echoing in my mind with every step I took along the dirt road back home.

Billy Rucker was waiting for me at the bend in the road near his house. He was carrying his battered baseball mitt, a familiar sight that sent a wave of relief through me. His smile was as easy as ever, his laughter quick to fill the quiet.

"You're looking good, Tob," he said, tossing the ball to me with a perfect arc. "Not bad for a guy who's been stuck inside for a year."

I caught the ball, grinning despite myself. "Feels good to be out, I'll tell you that much."

We began tossing the ball back and forth, our movements smooth and practiced, as if no time had passed.

"You missed a lot while you were gone," Billy said after a while. "Dr. King's been making waves.

Marches, speeches—he's got folks talking about things in a way I've never seen before."

I glanced at him, curious. "What do you mean?"

Billy paused, his mitt resting against his hip as he considered his words. "It's like... he's giving us something to believe in. Something to hope for. My daddy says it's dangerous, stirring folks up like that. But I think it's brave. I think it matters."

His voice was steady, but there was an intensity in his gaze that made me listen harder.

"What do you think will come of it?" I asked.

Billy shrugged, though his expression was thoughtful. "Change, maybe. Not fast, but enough to make a difference. Enough to make folks see things different—not just in Atlanta, or Washington, but even here in Pitney."

I nodded, the weight of his words settling over me. The struggles Billy and his family faced—the quiet, persistent barriers that shaped their lives—had always been there, even if I hadn't seen them clearly before. But hearing him speak now, I felt a deeper understanding beginning to take root.

Later that evening, as I sat on the porch of our house watching the sun dip below the horizon, I found myself thinking about what Reverend Tanner and Billy had said. Change wasn't easy—it wasn't quick, either. But it was possible. And, just maybe, the steps I was taking weren't just about me.

8

Redemption in Progress

Reintegrating into Pitney High School was like stepping into a spotlight I didn't ask for. Whispers followed me through the halls, hushed conversations that ended abruptly whenever I walked by. It didn't matter that a year had passed since my trial—my mistakes were still fresh in people's minds.

"Isn't that Toby Siler?" one girl muttered to her friend as I passed by.

"Yeah," the other replied, her voice barely above a whisper. "I heard he got sent away for stealing."

I kept my head down, gripping the strap of my backpack tightly as I made my way to class. But if there was one thing I'd learned at the Industrial Home, it was how to endure.

My first class was biology, taught by Mr. Franklin—a tall man with a kind smile and a passion for science that seemed to permeate every corner of his classroom. His lectures were lively, filled with anec-dotes and real-world connections that brought the subject to life.

"Science isn't just about memorizing facts," he said during one of his first lessons. "It's about understanding the world around you and asking questions that lead to discovery."

I wasn't much of a science enthusiast at the time, but something about Mr. Franklin's enthusiasm drew me in. The way he spoke about ecosystems, genetics, and the marvels of the human body made it impossible not to pay attention.

One day, after a particularly engaging lab where we'd dissected frogs to study their anatomy, Mr. Franklin pulled me aside as the other students filed out of the classroom.

"Toby, can I have a word?" he asked, his tone friendly but serious.

"Yes, sir," I said, pausing at the door.

He gestured for me to sit, taking the seat across from me. "You've got a good mind for this," he said, tapping the open textbook on the desk. "The way you approached today's lab showed focus and curiosity. Have you thought about pursuing science beyond high school?"

I blinked, caught off guard. "Not really, sir. I mean, I like it, but... I don't know if it's for me."

Mr. Franklin leaned forward, his expression thoughtful. "I'm not just talking about science as a subject. I'm talking about what it represents—understanding, problem-solving, making a difference. I've seen how you approach challenges, Toby. You don't just give up when things get hard. That's a quality that could take you far, especially in fields like medicine, engineering, or research."

"Medicine?" I repeated the word feeling foreign yet intriguing.

He nodded. "Have you ever thought about a career in health-care? Doctors, nurses, and scientists— they all start somewhere. And with your determination, I think you could be one of them."

I hesitated, the weight of his words settling over me. "I don't know, Mr. Franklin. I don't even know if I could get into college."

He smiled faintly, his confidence unwavering. "You don't have to have all the answers right now, Toby. But what you do need is a goal—a direction. And if you decide that medicine or science is something you want to pursue, I'll help you every step of the way."

His words stayed with me long after I left the classroom, echoing in my mind as I walked home. For the first time, I began to see a glimmer of possibility—a path forward that wasn't defined by my mistakes, but by what I could achieve. That mile home seemed like ten as my mind thought at a rapid pace. Me, a DOCTOR?

Sports had always been my refuge, and returning to the football field felt like reclaiming a part of myself I'd almost forgotten. Coach Miller, a grizzled man who seemed to live in his whistle, raised an eyebrow when I showed up at tryouts.

"Didn't think we'd see you back here," he said, his tone neutral but probing.

"I want to earn my place, Coach," I replied, meeting his gaze steadily.

His expression softened slightly, though he didn't let it show for long. "Alright, Siler. Let's see what you've got."

The tryouts were grueling—sprints, drills, and scrimmages that left my muscles screaming. But I gave it everything I had, fueled by a quiet determination to prove myself.

By the end of the week, I'd earned a spot on the team. It wasn't the starting lineup, but it was a start, and for the first time since my return, I felt a flicker of pride.

Laura had always been the steadying force in my life, and now, her presence was more important than ever. We fell into a rhythm, meeting after school at the diner on Main Street or walking down to Sinkhole Creek when the weather allowed.

One crisp autumn afternoon, as we sat on the creek bank skipping stones, she turned to me, her expression thoughtful.

"You've changed, Toby," she said simply.

I looked at her, unsure of how to respond. "Is that a good thing?"

Her lips curved into a small smile. "It's an incredibly good thing. But it's more than that—you're different, but you're still... you. Does that make sense?"

I nodded, a quiet warmth spreading through my chest. "You're the only one who makes me feel like I can be both," I admitted.

Her smile widened, and she took my hand in hers. "Then don't stop being that."

Billy Rucker and I still met on the dirt road when time allowed. His laughter was as easy as ever, but there was a seriousness beneath his words that reflected the changes both of us were going through.

"People in this town don't forget, do they?" I said one afternoon as we walked along the creek.

Billy shrugged. "It's not just Pitney—it's everywhere. But people can change, Toby. It's just slow. And you've got to make them see it."

"What about you?" I asked. "Do you think things will ever change for you, for your family?"

He paused; his gaze fixed on the horizon. "Dr. King's doing his part. And maybe if enough people listen, things will be better for the next generation. But for now, we've got to fight the fights we can."

His words lingered with me long after we parted ways, a reminder that redemption wasn't about proving myself—it was about understanding the struggles of others and finding ways to make things better.

That evening, as I sat at my desk attempting to sketch out a biology assignment, my thoughts kept drifting back to Mr. Franklin's words. Medicine. A doctor. The idea seemed impossibly far away, like a distant star I couldn't quite reach. But as I picked up my pencil and began writing, I felt the smallest ember of hope take root.

9

Forging Ahead

———◆◇◆———

The morning air carried the crisp promise of autumn as I stood on the football field, the grass wet with dew. Practice had just begun, and the scent of earth and sweat filled the air. I'd earned my place on the team after weeks of grueling tryouts, and while I was still relegated to the bench during games, I was determined to work my way up.

Coach Miller's voice boomed across the field, cutting through the fog. "Pick up the pace, Siler!

You think the other team's gonna wait for you to catch your breath?"

"Yes, sir!" I called back, pushing myself harder.

The drills were relentless—sprints, passes, tackles—but with each practice, I felt my body growing stronger, my confidence inching closer to where it had once been. The camaraderie with my teammates, once strained, began to grow as they saw the effort I was putting in.

"You've got heart, Siler," one of the linebackers said after practice, clapping me on the back.

"Keep it up."

It was a small gesture, but it carried more weight than he probably realized.

As part of my probation, Reverend Tanner had arranged for me to help with community projects around town. Most days, it meant cleaning up the park, painting fences, or assisting with odd jobs at the church.

At first, I approached the work with a sense of duty, eager to check off the hours and move on. But as the weeks went by, something shifted. The people I helped—elderly neighbors who needed their yards raked; parents grateful for the freshly painted playground equipment— began to see me differently.

One Saturday, as I finished repairing a broken bench in the park, an older man approached me.

"You did good work here, son," he said, his weathered face breaking into a smile. "This bench's been here longer than I have, and it means a lot to see it taken care of."

"Thank you, sir," I replied, my chest tightening with a mix of pride and humility.

Moments like that reminded me that redemption wasn't about what I did for myself—it was about what I could do for others.

Balancing football, community service, and academics was no easy feat, but I threw myself into my studies with the same determination I brought to the field. Inspired by Mr. Franklin's encouragement, I began to see biology not just as a subject, but as a window into a future I'd never considered before.

One evening after class, I stayed late to work on a lab assignment. Mr. Franklin noticed my focus and pulled up a chair beside me.

"You're getting the hang of this," he said, nodding at the neatly labeled diagrams in my notebook. "How's it feel?"

"Honestly?" I said, glancing up at him. "It feels... good. Like maybe I could actually do something with this."

He smiled, his confidence in me unwavering. "You can, Toby. But remember—it's not just about what you're learning here. It's about what you're willing to do with it."

His words stayed with me as I packed up my things and headed home.

By the time football season reached its midpoint, my hard work had earned me a spot in the starting lineup. The first time I stepped onto the field under the Friday night lights, the roar of the crowd sent a surge of adrenaline through me.

The game was a nail-biter, every play a test of our endurance and teamwork. When the final whistle blew and the scoreboard showed our victory, the cheers from the stands felt like a weight lifting off my shoulders.

After the game, as the team celebrated on the sidelines, I caught sight of Mama and Daddy in the crowd. Mama was clapping, her face glowing with pride. Daddy's expression was more reserved, but when our eyes met, he gave me a small nod—a silent acknowledgment that spoke louder than words.

It was a late Saturday afternoon when Reverend Tanner called me into his office after our weekly meeting. The setting sun cast long shadows across the room, the warm light filtering through the stained-glass windows behind him. He leaned back in his chair, his hands folded neatly on his desk, and studied me with that thoughtful, measured look he always had.

"Toby," he began, his voice calm yet purposeful, "how do you feel about standing in front of a crowd?"

I blinked, caught off guard. "I guess... It depends on the crowd. Why do you ask?"

A small smile tugged at the corner of his mouth. "I'd like you to share your story with the congregation tomorrow during Sunday service."

My stomach dropped. "You want me to—what?"

He chuckled softly, his gaze steady but kind. "I want you to speak, Toby. About your journey, the lessons you've learned, and how you're working to turn things around. The folks here have watched you grow up—they've seen your highs and your lows. But what they haven't seen is the heart of the young man you're becoming."

I swallowed hard, the weight of his request settling over me. "I don't know, Reverend. I'm not much of a speaker, and... what if they're not ready to hear from me?"

Reverend Tanner leaned forward, his tone soft but firm. "This isn't about them—it's about you. Standing up and sharing your truth isn't easy, but it's a step toward showing the world, and yourself, who you really are. And you don't have to do it alone—I'll be right there with you."

Finally, I nodded, though my palms were already sweating at the thought of tomorrow. "Alright. I'll do it."

The next morning, the church was packed. Mama and Daddy sat near the front, their hands folded tightly in their laps, while Robbie had managed to find a seat in the back row just before the service began. Laura also came to hear me and sat near the front to lend encouragement.

When Reverend Tanner called my name and stepped aside to let me take the pulpit, my heart felt like it might beat out of my chest.

I began nervously, introducing myself and speaking of my mistakes. As I continued, I talked about my time at the Industrial Home, the lessons I'd learned in humility and discipline, and the importance of second chances.

When I finished, the room was silent for a moment that felt like an eternity. Then, slowly, the sound of applause filled the space—not thunderous, but warm and genuine.

As I returned to my seat, Reverend Tanner stepped up to the pulpit with a calm confidence that filled the room. He opened his Bible to Romans 5:8 and read aloud, *"But God demonstrates His own love for us in this: While we were still sinners, Christ died for us."*

"The beauty of redemption," he began, "is that it isn't earned—it's given. God doesn't wait for us to be perfect or to prove ourselves worthy. He meets us where we are, in our brokenness, and offers us a chance to begin again."

Reverend Tanner continued, tying my story into a larger theme of grace and growth. "Let this be a reminder," he concluded, "that no matter who we are or what we've done, redemption is always possible. It's not about erasing the past—it's about rewriting the future. And that, my friends, is the heart of God's love for us."

10

Rising Above

The winter chill settled over Pitney, frosting the edges of windows and turning the dirt roads as hard as stone. At the start of the season, I found myself standing at a crossroads—not a literal one, but a figurative one that seemed to widen with every decision I made. Redemption wasn't something I could achieve overnight, and though progress had been steady, there were moments when doubt threatened to creep back in.

Pitney had begun to soften toward me, but not everyone was ready to let go of the past. Whispers still lingered at the grocery store, at the diner, and even in church—the faint echoes of skepticism that reminded me how much work I still had to do.

One Saturday morning, as I raked leaves in Mrs. Evans's yard—a part of my ongoing community service—a neighbor stopped on the sidewalk to watch me. I glanced up briefly, recognizing Mr. Harper, whose sharp comments and narrowed eyes had been a constant presence during my youth.

"Doing a little cleanup, are we?" He asked, his tone carrying the faintest trace of mockery.

"Yes, sir," I replied evenly, continuing my work.

He lingered, the tension between us palpable, until Mrs. Evans emerged onto the porch with a smile.

"Toby's been such a help these past few weeks," she said, her voice warm and genuine. "Not many young men would give up their weekends like this. I don't know how I'd manage without him."

Mr. Harper's expression shifted, though he didn't say anything more before walking away. The brief encounter wasn't a victory, but it felt like another step forward—a quiet affirmation that actions spoke louder than words.

With Mr. Franklin's guidance, I had begun seriously considering my future, even if the idea of college still felt daunting. He had encouraged me to apply to Mercer University—a school he said had a strong biology program and a history of giving students like me a chance.

"You've got what it takes, Toby," he said one afternoon as we worked together in the lab. "You just need to believe it."

His confidence was contagious, and as the application process loomed closer, I found myself daring to hope—not just for acceptance, but for the chance to prove that I was capable of more than anyone had imagined.

The day of my high school graduation dawned clear and bright, the early summer sunlight streaming through my bedroom window like a promise. I rolled out of bed with a mix of excitement and apprehension, my stomach twisting with the weight of the day. It wasn't about walking across the stage—it was about what the moment represented, the culmination of years of hard work, setbacks, and second chances.

As I pulled on my cap and gown, Mama hovered nearby, fussing over every detail.

"Toby, stand still," she said, adjusting the tassel with a proud but trembling hand. "You look so handsome—just like your daddy on his graduation day."

I smiled faintly, the comparison carrying a weight I wasn't sure I could live up to. "Thanks, Mama. It means a lot."

The auditorium buzzed with nervous energy as families took their seats, their conversations blending into a symphony of anticipation. The scent of fresh flowers mingled with the faint aroma of varnished wood, creating an atmosphere both celebratory and nostalgic.

We filed in one by one, the tassels on our caps swaying with every step. As I walked toward my seat, I caught glimpses of familiar faces in the crowd—Mama and Daddy sitting near the front, their expressions a mix of pride and emotion. Robbie had managed to snag a spot toward the back, his grin already shining from across the room. Laura was seated a few rows away, her auburn hair catching the light as she waved subtly.

Principal Adams began the ceremony with a speech that spoke of resilience, growth, and the promise of the future. Her words resonated deeply, a reminder that each of us had faced challenges along the way—and for me, those challenges had shaped the very core of who I was becoming.

When my name was called, I stepped onto the stage with measured strides, the lights washing over me as the applause swelled. The moment felt surreal, a kaleidoscope of emotions swirling within me—gratitude, relief, and a quiet pride I hadn't dared to fully embrace until now.

Principal Adams shook my hand firmly, her smile wide. "Congratulations, Toby. You've earned this."

"Thank you," I said, my voice steady despite the lump in my throat.

As I turned to face the crowd, my gaze swept over the sea of faces. Mama was dabbing at her eyes with a handkerchief, her smile radiant despite the tears. Daddy nodded slightly when our eyes met, his approval as solid and unwavering as the man himself. Robbie cheered from the back, his whistle piercing through the applause, while Laura's grin shone like a beacon.

Returning to my seat, diploma in hand, I felt the weight of the moment—not as a burden, but as a triumph.

Back home, Mama had turned our modest kitchen into a feast fit for royalty. Platters of fried chicken, mashed potatoes, collard greens, and cornbread covered every inch of the table, while a pecan pie sat cooling on the counter.

Robbie clapped me on the back as I walked in, his grin wide. "You did it, Tob. You didn't just graduate—you showed them all what you're made of."

Daddy, standing in the corner with his arms crossed, raised his glass of sweet tea. "Here's to you, son. Keep proving them wrong."

We ate, laughed, and reminisced about the journey that had brought us to this moment. It wasn't just a celebration—it was a recognition of how far we'd all come together.

That evening, as the stars blinked into view above the clay hills, I sat on the porch swing with Laura beside me, the air filled with the soft hum of crickets.

"You've come a long way, Toby," she said, her voice steady yet warm.

I nodded, my thoughts drifting between the past and the future. "Yeah. But there's still a lot to do."

She smiled, resting her hand lightly on mine. "That's the good part—the journey's just starting." I didn't know exactly where the road would lead, but for the first time, I was ready to walk it.

11

A New Horizon

—◦◦◦—

The morning I left Pitney, the air was thick with the scent of honeysuckle and freshly turned soil, as if the town itself was bidding me a bittersweet farewell. The bus idled at the station, its engine rumbling softly like a giant taking a nap. Mama was fussing over my suitcase, double-checking the clasps for the third time.

"You've got everything you need?" She asked, her hands flitting over my shirt collar, my hair, and my face, as though trying to memorize me.

"Yes, Mama," I said, smiling gently to reassure her.

Robbie stood a few steps away, hands shoved in his pockets as he surveyed the scene. "You're gonna do just fine, Tob," he said, his grin equal parts encouragement and mischief. "Don't let those city folks get too full of themselves. Show 'em what Pitney's made of."

"I'll do my best," I replied, my chest tightening at the thought of leaving him behind.

Daddy's approach was quieter, his footsteps steady as he extended a firm hand. "Proud of you," he said simply. "Make the most of this chance."

Laura was the last person I hugged before boarding the bus, and when her arms wrapped around me, the weight of what we were leaving behind settled heavily between us.

"I'm going to miss you so much," she said, her voice soft but steady.

"Me too," I replied, pulling back slightly to look into her eyes. "But we'll make it work. I know we will."

For a moment, we stood in silence, the sounds of the bus and the faint chatter of the station fading into the background. Then, without hesitation, I whispered, "I love you, Laura."

Her lips parted in surprise, but the soft smile that followed lit up her whole face. "I love you too, Toby," she said, her voice carrying a certainty that filled me with warmth.

It wasn't until I boarded the bus and settled into a seat near the window that it hit me. For the first time in my life, I was leaving Pitney—not just for a day or a week, but for something bigger, something unknown. As the bus pulled away and the familiar sights of home blurred into the distance, I felt both a weight and a lightness I couldn't quite explain.

Around the same time I was packing my bags for Mercer, Laura received her acceptance letter to Abraham Baldwin Agricultural College in Tifton, Georgia. It was a two-year program where she would pursue a degree in business administration—a path she had talked about for years but never quite believed she could follow.

She called me the day the letter arrived, her voice bubbling with excitement.

"Toby, guess what!"

"What's going on?" I asked, smiling at the happiness radiating through the phone.

"I got in!" she exclaimed. "Abraham Baldwin! I'm going to study business administration!"

"That's amazing, Laura!" I replied, the joy in her voice contagious. "I'm so proud of you."

"Thank you," she said, her tone softening. "It feels real now, you know? Like I'm finally taking control of my future."

"You are," I said firmly. "And you're going to do great. Just remember—keep that fire going, no matter what."

Her laughter rang out on the other end of the line, light and full of promise. "You're good at this pep talk thing," she teased.

We talked for nearly an hour, sharing dreams and fears about the paths we were about to take. Though the distance between Tifton and Macon seemed daunting, we both knew it was a necessary step—one that would strengthen, not weaken, the bond we'd built over the years.

Arriving at Mercer University was like stepping into a different world. The campus buzzed with energy, students crisscrossing the wide green lawns with books in hand, their conversations blending into a symphony of ambition and excitement.

My dormitory was a modest brick building, its walls worn but sturdy. My roommate, Evan, was a wiry kid from Savannah with a quick wit and a talent for finding humor in almost anything.

"You're from Pitney?" he asked as we unpacked our things. "I don't think I've even seen it on a map."

"Most people haven't," I said with a grin. "But it's home."

Evan nodded thoughtfully, his gaze momentarily distant. "Well, here's to new beginnings," he said, raising an imaginary glass.

Every few weeks, Laura's letters arrived, her handwriting neat and slightly slanted, as though each word carried its own momentum.

Toby, one letter began, *being at Abraham Baldwin is amazing and intimidating all at the same time. I'm learning so much, but sometimes I feel like I'm drowning in coursework and expectations. But then I think of you and how you always tell me to keep the fire going, and I find my way back.*

In another letter, she shared her feelings with a vulnerability that made me hold my breath as I read:

I think about that moment at the bus station a lot—when you told me you loved me. Hearing those words, Toby, made me feel braver than I've ever felt in my whole life. I love you too, more than I can ever put into words. Knowing you're out there, chasing your dreams, makes me feel like I can do anything.

Her words were a lifeline, grounding me in the midst of the whirlwind that college had become. In one letter, she enclosed a small photograph of Sinkhole Creek at sunset, the colors vivid and warm.

I thought you might like a little piece of home to keep with you, she wrote.

I kept her letters tucked safely in a shoebox under my bed, pulling them out whenever the weight of college life felt too heavy.

One crisp autumn evening, as I walked back to my dorm after a long day of classes and lab work, I stopped by the campus fountain. The water sparkled under the soft glow of the lampposts, its gentle rhythm a soothing backdrop to my thoughts.

For the first time since arriving at Mercer, I felt a sense of belonging—not just to the campus, but to the path I was carving for myself. The struggles, the uncertainties, and the victories—all of it was shaping me into someone I was beginning to recognize and respect.

As I sat on the edge of the fountain, the cool stone beneath my hands, I whispered a quiet promise to myself: I would make this work. For Mama and Daddy, for Robbie and Billy, for Mr. Franklin and Reverend Tanner—but most importantly, for me and for Laura, who believed in me even when I didn't believe in myself.

12

Bridges to the Future

T he pace of life at Mercer began to shift with the changing seasons. As winter gave way to spring, the campus came alive with the sound of laughter and the buzz of students enjoying the warm sun on the green. For me, the transition was less about the weather and more about finding my rhythm—a balance between rigorous coursework, late-night study sessions, and the quiet moments I carved out to reflect on how far I'd come.

Dr. Porter's words echoed in my mind often: *"You've got potential, Toby. And potential is a powerful thing—if you're willing to put in the work."* Those words became a kind of mantra for me, a steady reminder to keep pushing forward even when the challenges felt insurmountable.

One of the first friendships I formed outside of my roommate Evan was with a fellow biology student named Angela. She was sharp and outspoken, with a quick laugh and a determination that rivaled my own. We often found ourselves paired up for lab work, her efficiency balancing out my careful, deliberate approach.

"You're way too patient with this stuff," she teased one afternoon as I meticulously measured a solution for an experiment.

"And you're way too quick," I shot back with a grin.

The banter was light, but there was a mutual respect that grew with each lab session. Angela had a way of making me see things differently—not just in science, but in life.

"You know," she said one day as we packed up our equipment, "you've got this calm determination that's kind of impressive. Like, you just keep going, no matter what."

I shrugged, her words catching me off guard. "I guess I've had a lot of practice."

She tilted her head, studying me for a moment. "Whatever it is, don't lose it. The world needs people who don't give up."

As my confidence grew, I began seeking out opportunities beyond the classroom. One day, I noticed a flyer on the bulletin board outside the science building: *Research Assistant Needed— Apply Within.*

The idea intrigued me, and after a brief meeting with the professor overseeing the project, I found myself joining a small team of students working on water quality research in nearby streams. It was hands-on work—collecting samples, analyzing data, and presenting findings— and it ignited a passion I hadn't fully realized was there.

The experience wasn't without its challenges. There were late nights in the lab, unexpected setbacks in the field, and moments of doubt that threatened to derail me. But each obstacle was an opportunity to learn, to adapt, and to prove to myself that I belonged in this world of discovery.

One particularly long day ended with the welcome sight of a letter waiting in my dorm mailbox.

The familiar slant of Laura's handwriting brought an instant smile to my face.

Toby, it began, *I've been thinking about how much we've both grown since we left Pitney. Being at Abraham Baldwin has shown me that I'm capable of so much more than I ever imagined, and I see the same in you. I'm so proud of everything you're doing at Mercer. It feels like we're both building bridges to the future—different paths but heading in the same direction.*

Her words were a reminder of the bond we shared, a connection that distance couldn't diminish. As I read her letter under the soft glow of the desk lamp, I felt a renewed sense of purpose, knowing that everything I was working for wasn't just for me—it was for the life we were building together, piece by piece.

One of the biggest lessons I learned that year was how to embrace uncertainty. Whether it was navigating complex lab work, presenting findings to a room full of professors, or figuring out how to budget my time and energy, I came to understand that growth often came from the most uncomfortable moments.

Dr. Porter noticed the shift in me. "You're getting the hang of this," he said after one particularly challenging presentation. "You're not just keeping up anymore—you're standing out."

The words filled me with a quiet pride, but they also reminded me of the responsibility that came with my ambitions. I wasn't just representing myself at Mercer—I was carrying the lessons and values of Pitney with me, bridging the gap between where I came from and where I was headed.

The semester ended with a trip back home to Pitney, the familiar sights and sounds wrapping around me like a warm embrace. One afternoon, I found myself at Sinkhole Creek, the water glistening under the golden light of the setting sun. Laura joined me, her laughter filling the air as we skipped stones across the surface.

"I missed this," she said, her voice soft but full of emotion.

"Me too," I replied, my gaze lingering on the ripples spreading across the water. "But I think... I'm starting to figure it out. How to take everything I've learned here and bring it with me, wherever I go."

She smiled, her hand finding mine. "You've always had it in you, Toby. You just needed to see it for yourself."

As the sun dipped below the horizon, painting the sky in hues of orange and pink, I felt a sense of peace I hadn't known in years. The bridges I was building—to my future, to Laura, to the person I wanted to become—were no longer just dreams. They were real, solid, and ready to carry me wherever I chose to go.

13

Trials and Triumphs

The beginning of my second year at Mercer felt different—less like stepping into the unknown and more like settling into a rhythm I could claim as my own. The campus, with its sprawling green lawns and brick pathways, had become a place of familiarity and purpose. Yet, with each step forward, the challenges only seemed to grow.

Dr. Porter's biology lectures became more intense, delving into the complexities of genetics and cellular processes that left my head spinning more often than not. The research team I'd joined the year before had expanded its scope, demanding longer hours in the lab and more intricate fieldwork. And while the workload often felt overwhelming, there was a part of me that thrived on the pressure—the knowledge that every challenge was a step closer to proving I belonged.

One afternoon, as I stood in the lab analyzing a set of water samples, Angela strode in with her usual energy, her ponytail swaying as she set her books down.

"Toby, you've got to see this," she said, her voice brimming with excitement as she handed me a report.

The data revealed a significant finding in our research—something unexpected and potentially groundbreaking.

"This could change everything," she said, her eyes shining.

But with the discovery came a new challenge: presenting our findings at an academic conference in Atlanta—a prospect that both thrilled and terrified me.

Dr. Porter encouraged me to take the lead on the presentation. "You've earned this, Toby," he said, his tone firm but supportive. "This is your chance to step up."

The weeks leading up to the conference were a whirlwind of preparation. Angela and I worked late nights perfecting our presentation, rehearsing until we could recite the data in our sleep. By the time the day arrived, I felt as ready as I'd ever be.

Standing before a room full of scientists and students, my palms slick with nerves, I took a deep breath and began. As I spoke, the initial tremor in my voice steadied, replaced by a confidence I hadn't realized I possessed. When I finished, the applause was genuine, and the questions that followed showed a keen interest in our work.

Dr. Porter's words after the presentation stayed with me: "You didn't just deliver the data—you told a story. That's what makes great science. Well done, Toby."

Amid the chaos of academics and research, letters from home continued to be my anchor. Mama wrote about the changing seasons in Pitney, the way the pecan trees seemed to glow in the golden light of autumn. Robbie's updates were filled with humor, his tales of small-town antics a welcome reprieve from the intensity of college life.

And then there were Laura's letters, each one a treasure I read and reread on the nights when the weight of my responsibilities felt heaviest.

Toby, one began, *I can't stop thinking about the amazing work you're doing. Every time I feel overwhelmed here at Abraham Baldwin, I remind myself that you're out there tackling things ten times harder—and doing it brilliantly. I love you, and I know you're going to change the world someday.*

Her belief in me was a light I carried through the darkest days, a reminder that the bridges we were building together were strong enough to span any distance.

While academics consumed most of my time, football remained a vital outlet. The camaraderie of the team and the thrill of the game were a reminder of the grit and determination I'd carried with me from Pitney.

But the season wasn't without its challenges. A midseason injury sidelined me for weeks, leaving me grappling with frustration and doubt. Watching from the sidelines as my teammates pushed forward was both inspiring and humbling.

"Setbacks are just setups for comebacks," Coach Miller told me during one of our talks. "Focus on recovery, and when you're ready, hit the field like you've never left."

Those words became my mantra as I threw myself into physical therapy, determined to return stronger than before. By the time I rejoined the team, the sense of triumph was sweeter than any victory on the scoreboard.

The highlight of the semester came on a crisp October weekend when Laura made the trip from Tifton to visit me at Mercer. Seeing her standing on campus, her auburn hair catching the light and her smile wide, felt like a breath of fresh air.

We spent the day exploring the campus, sharing stories of our respective journeys and imagining what the future might hold.

"This place suits you, Toby," she said as we sat by the campus fountain. "You've grown so much here—you're becoming the person you were always meant to be."

Her words brought a lump to my throat, and I reached for her hand, holding it tightly. "None of this would've been possible without you, Laura. You've always believed in me, even when I didn't believe in myself."

She smiled, her eyes glistening with emotion. "That's because I've always known how amazing you are."

As we sat there, the world seemed to fade away, leaving only the quiet rhythm of the fountain and the steady beat of our hearts.

As the semester drew to a close, I found myself reflecting on how much had changed—not just at Mercer, but within me. The trials I'd faced, the bridges I'd built, and the triumphs I'd achieved had all shaped me into someone I was beginning to recognize as strong, capable, and ready for whatever came next.

The road ahead was still uncertain, but for the first time, that uncertainty felt less like a barrier and more like an adventure waiting to unfold.

14

The Weight of Choices

---⦿---

The start of my third year at Mercer brought a strange mix of confidence and unease. I had found my rhythm in college life, built bridges to friendships and opportunities, and begun carving a path toward the future I wanted. But with that growth came a weight I couldn't ignore—a constant reminder that every step I took carried consequences not just for me, but for the people who believed in me.

Balancing my course load with research, football, and apart-time job at the campus library was no easy feat. Late nights turned into early mornings as I tried to stay on top of everything, my planner filled with scribbled notes and reminders that seemed to multiply by the day.

"You're going to run yourself into the ground," Angela said one afternoon as we packed up after a lab session.

"I don't have much choice," I replied with a shrug. "There's too much at stake to slow down now."

She studied me for a moment, her expression thoughtful. "Just don't forget to breathe every once in a while. The world won't fall apart if you take a break."

I nodded, though her words didn't fully sink in until much later.

One crisp October morning, a letter from Mama arrived, her familiar handwriting bringing an instant smile to my face.

Toby, it began, *I was thinking about you the other day when I was baking pecan pies for the church fundraiser. It reminded me of when you were little, always sneaking a bite of the pecan filling before it went into the oven. You've always been someone who goes after what they want, and I know that determination will take you far. Just remember, no matter where you go or what you do, you'll always have a home here in Pitney.*

Her words felt like a warm hug, a reminder of the roots that grounded me even as I reached for new heights.

The semester reached a turning point when I was offered an internship at a local hospital—an opportunity that aligned perfectly with my goal of pursuing a career in medicine. But accepting the internship meant cutting back on other responsibilities, including my part-time job and football, both of which had become integral parts of my college experience.

I wrestled with the decision for days, the weight of it pressing heavily on my shoulders. One evening, I found myself sitting on the edge of my bed, the internship offer letter crumpled in my hand as I stared at the floor.

"You look like you're about to break," Evan said from across the room, his voice pulling me out of my thoughts.

"I just don't know what to do," I admitted. "It feels like no matter what I choose, I'm letting something go."

He leaned back in his chair, his expression serious. "Sounds to me like you already know the answer—you're just scared to say it out loud."

His words hit me like a punch to the gut, but they were exactly what I needed to hear. That night, I called Laura, knowing she'd understand.

"I'm scared," I confessed, the words tumbling out before I could stop them. "What if I mess this up?"

Her voice was calm but firm. "Toby, you've faced bigger challenges than this. You know what you need to do—just trust yourself."

With her encouragement echoing in my ears, I made my decision. The next day, I accepted the internship, knowing it was the right step toward the future I wanted.

Stepping into the hospital for my first day as an intern was both exhilarating and nerve wracking. The sterile scent of disinfectant and the steady hum of activity filled the air as I navigated the bustling hallways.

My supervisor, Dr. Bennett was a seasoned physician with a no-nonsense demeanor and a wealth of knowledge. "This isn't going to be easy," she said during our first meeting. "But if you're willing to put in the work, you'll learn more here than you ever imagined."

The days were long and demanding, filled with tasks that tested both my stamina and my resolve. I shadowed doctors during rounds, took notes during patient consultations, and even assisted with small tasks like charting and organizing records.

It was exhausting, but it was also deeply rewarding—a glimpse into the world I had dreamed of joining since my conversations with Mr. Franklin back in Pitney.

On one of my rare days off, Laura and I managed to carveout time for a phone call that felt like a lifeline.

"I wish I could be there to see you in action," she said, her voice filled with admiration.

"Trust me, it's not as glamorous as it sounds," I replied with a chuckle. "But it's worth it. Every second."

She paused, and I could hear the faint sound of pages turning in the background. "Toby," she said finally, "I'm so proud of you. You're doing something amazing—not just for yourself, but for everyone whosoever believed in you."

Her words stayed with me long after the call ended, a beacon of light that carried me through the toughest days.

As the semester drew to a close, I found myself reflecting on the choices I'd made—the bridges I'd built, the sacrifices I'd embraced, and the challenges I'd overcome. The road ahead was still uncertain, but for the first time, I felt ready to face it, no matter what it held.

The weight of my choices wasn't a burden—it was a testament to how far I'd come and how much further I could go.

15

The Road to Becoming

By the time I started my second semester as an intern at the hospital, the bustling hallways and rhythmic hum of activity had become as familiar to me as the streets of Pitney. There was a comfort in the routine—a sense of purpose that seemed to anchor me even on the most hectic days.

Dr. Bennett, my supervisor, had a knack for pushing me past my limits in ways I hadn't expected. Her feedback was sharp and direct, but it was always paired with encouragement that kept me striving for more.

"You've got potential, Toby," she said one afternoon as we finished rounds. "But potential doesn't mean much unless you act on it. Show me what you're capable of."

Her words stayed with me long after our conversation, pushing me to dig deeper—to ask more questions, to take more initiative, to find the balance between confidence and humility.

One particularly chaotic day tested that balance in ways I hadn't anticipated. It started with a simple task—retrieving supplies from the storage room—but quickly spiraled into a crisis when a nurse rushed into the hallway, her voice strained.

"We need extra hands in the ER," she said. "Can you help?"

I hesitated for a split second before nodding. Following her into the crowded ER, I found myself thrust into a whirlwind of motion—doctors shouting orders, nurses rushing between patients, the steady beep of monitors blending into the background.

I assisted where I could, my heart pounding as I followed instructions and tried to stay out of the way. When the chaos finally settled, Dr. Bennett approached me, her expression unreadable.

"You kept your head when things got intense," she said. "That's not something everyone can do."

I nodded, the adrenaline still coursing through me. "It was overwhelming, but... I couldn't just stand by."

Her faint smile carried a note of approval. "Good instincts, Toby. Keep honing them."

Later that week, a letter from Laura arrived, her neat handwriting filling the page with warmth and encouragement.

Toby, it began, *I heard about your ER experience from your last letter, and I can't stop thinking about how incredible you are. The way you stepped up and kept going even when things got tough—it's inspiring. You're going to be an amazing doctor someday, and I can't wait to see everything you accomplish.*

Her belief in me was a steadying force, a reminder that no matter how difficult the road ahead seemed, I wasn't walking it alone.

Meanwhile, my coursework at Mercer continued to challenge and shape me. One particular project in my molecular biology class stood out—not just for its complexity, but for the way it opened my eyes to the possibilities within the field of research.

Angela and I partnered up for the project, our dynamic in the lab once again proving to be a perfect balance.

"This is it, Toby," she said as we presented our findings to the class. "This is the kind of work that changes things."

Her enthusiasm reignited my passion for discovery, reminding me why I had chosen this path in the first place.

Toward the end of the semester, Dr. Porter pulled me aside after class, his expression contemplative.

"You've come a long way since you first stepped into my classroom," he said. "But there's something I need you to understand—the road you're on isn't just about reaching the finish line. It's about what you learn along the way, about how you adapt and grow with every challenge."

I nodded, his words resonating deeply. "I know it's going to be hard, but... I think I'm ready for it."

His smile carried a note of pride. "You've already proven that, Toby. Keep proving it—to yourself and to the world."

As I sat on the steps outside the hospital one evening, the sunset painting the sky in hues of orange and pink, I found myself reflecting on the journey so far. The trials, the triumphs, the moments of doubt and determination—they were all shaping me into someone I was beginning to understand and respect.

The road to becoming wasn't about achieving a goal—it was about embracing the process, the growth, the lessons that came with every step forward.

For the first time, I felt not just ready to face the future—I felt ready to become it.

16

Building Together

———◆◇◆———

T he air in Tifton carried a bittersweet warmth as Laura stepped onto the stage to receive her diploma. The auditorium buzzed with applause as the graduates crossed one by one, their caps and gowns swaying with the movement. When Laura's name was announced, the pride radiating from her family in the audience was palpable, their cheers rising above the rest.

Her auburn hair shimmered under the bright lights as she shook hands with the dean, her smile steady but emotional. For Laura, this wasn't just a ceremony—it was the culmination of years of determination, hard work, and the quiet resolve that had carried her forward even when the path seemed uncertain.

After the ceremony, as her family gathered around her, Laura's gaze lingered on the diploma in her hands. It wasn't just a piece of paper—it was a symbol of everything she had worked for, a bridge to the future she had dreamed of building.

Graduating with a degree in Business Administration opened new doors for Laura, and as she searched for opportunities, one possibility stood out—a position as a Business Office Manager at a growing company in Macon. The idea of starting her career while being closer to Toby was an opportunity she couldn't ignore.

Her first day on the job was nerve-wracking but exciting. The office buzzed with activity, the sound of ringing phones and muffled conversations blending into a rhythm she quickly adapted to. Laura's supervisor, Ms. Gaines was a sharp and organized woman who recognized Laura's potential immediately.

"You've got a good head on your shoulders," she said during their first meeting. "This role is going to challenge you, but I think you'll handle it just fine."

Laura threw herself into the work, her natural knack for organization and leadership helping her navigate the fast-paced environment. Her responsibilities ranged from managing schedules to coordinating office operations, and while the workload was heavy, she thrived under the pressure.

One evening, as she sat at her desk reviewing reports, a text from Toby lit up her phone: *How's my superstar doing?*

Her smile stretched wide as she replied: *Busy but good. I'll tell you all about it tonight.*

Being in Macon meant that Laura and Toby could spend more time together—a gift they cherished after years of long-distance. On evenings when Toby wasn't at the hospital or buried in coursework, they explored the city, from its bustling downtown streets to its quieter parks where they could simply enjoy each other's company.

One sunny afternoon, they sat on a bench overlooking the river, the gentle breeze rustling the leaves. Laura's head rested lightly against Toby's shoulder as they watched the sunlight glint off the water.

"You know," Laura said softly, "I never thought life would take us here—to this moment, this place. But I'm so glad it did."

Toby smiled, his hand wrapping around hers. "Me too. It feels like we're starting to build something real—together."

Her gaze lifted to meet his, her eyes shimmering with emotion. "We are, Toby. And I can't wait to see where it takes us."

As the weeks passed, their routines began to merge—Laura's days in the office, Toby's nights at the hospital, and the moments they carved out for each other in between. They supported one another in ways both big and small, from sharing advice over dinner to cheering each other on during difficult days.

One evening, as they sat on the couch surrounded by takeout boxes, Laura turned to Toby with a thoughtful expression.

"Do you ever think about what's next?" she asked. "Not just for us, but for everything we're building."

Toby nodded, his gaze steady. "All the time. But I think...as long as we keep moving forward, together, we'll figure it out."

Her smile widened, and she leaned in to kiss him softly. "I love you, Toby."

"I love you too, Laura," he replied, his voice filled with certainty.

Their story wasn't about individual success—it was about the quiet, steady work of building something meaningful together. Through every challenge, every triumph, and every moment of doubt, Laura and Toby found strength in each other, their bond growing stronger with each passing day.

The road ahead was still full of uncertainties, but they faced it with the unwavering belief that together, they could handle whatever came their way.

17

Crossing Paths

The steady rhythm of life in Macon brought a sense of stability that Toby and Laura hadn't experienced in years. Their days were busy and often exhausting, but the moments they shared in between carried a warmth that reminded them why they had worked so hard to get here.

Laura had quickly settled into her role as a Business Office Manager, her knack for organization and leadership earning her the respect of her colleagues. Toby, meanwhile, balanced the demands of his internship and coursework, finding in Laura a source of encouragement that never wavered.

One sunny afternoon, as they drove through Macon on their way back from errands, Toby suddenly slowed the car and turned onto an overgrown side street.

"Where are we going?" Laura asked, her curiosity piqued.

Toby didn't answer immediately, his eyes scanning the road ahead. "There's something I want to show you," he said finally.

As the car came to a stop, Laura looked out the window to see a crumbling building surrounded by a tangle of weeds and grass. The Macon Industrial Home for Boys stood silent and abandoned, its once imposing facade now marred by broken windows and peeling paint.

Laura turned to Toby, her expression softening. "This is where you..."

"Yeah," he said, cutting the engine. "This is where I spent that year."

They climbed out of the car, the crunch of gravel beneath their feet the only sound as they approached the building. Toby's gaze lingered on the broken front doors, the faded sign above them barely legible.

"It's strange," he said after a moment, his voice quiet. "When I was here, it felt like the end of the world. But now... I don't know. It's like looking at a ghost of who I used to be."

Laura reached for his hand, her grip firm but gentle. "You've come so far since then, Toby. This place doesn't define you—it never did."

They sat on the hood of the car, the sun casting long shadows over the overgrown yard. Toby's eyes remained fixed on the building as memories flooded back—the harsh dormitory lights, the grueling days in the industrial shop, the moments of defiance and determination that had carried him through.

"It was tough," he said, his voice steady but tinged with emotion. "There were days I didn't think I'd make it. But in a way, this place saved me. It forced me to face who I was and decide who I wanted to be."

Laura leaned against him, her head resting on his shoulder. "You're one of the strongest people I know, Toby. And it's because you've faced things most people can't even imagine."

He glanced at her, a faint smile tugging at his lips. "I couldn't have done it without people like you, though. You and Reverend Tanner, Mr. Franklin, my family... you all gave me something to fight for."

They sat in silence for a while, the weight of the moment settling over them. The building stood as a testament to a past that had shaped Toby, but it was the future he and Laura were building together that filled the air with promise.

Despite the challenges, both Toby and Laura found moments of triumph in their respective worlds. For Laura, it was securing a new client for her company—a deal she had worked tirelessly to negotiate. Her coworkers celebrated with applause and congratulations, but it was Toby's reaction that meant the most.

"That's amazing, Laura!" he said when she shared the news over dinner. "I'm so proud of you."

For Toby, it was successfully completing a particularly complex case study at the hospital—a moment that earned him praise from Dr. Bennett and reaffirmed his path toward medicine. "You're making strides, Toby," Dr. Bennett said, her tone steady but warm. "Keep it up—you're going to go far."

With their schedules becoming increasingly demanding, Toby and Laura decided to take a much needed weekend getaway to the countryside outside Macon. The fresh air and quiet surroundings were a welcome reprieve from the constant buzz of city life.

They spent the days hiking through trails lined with towering trees and the evenings sitting by a crackling fire, the stars above them sparkling like diamonds.

"You know," Laura said one night as they sat wrapped in blankets, "sometimes I think about what it would be like to have this kind of peace every day."

Toby nodded; his gaze fixed on the firelight. "Me too. But I think... the peace means more when you've worked hard to earn it."

She smiled, resting her head against his shoulder. "I think you're right. And I think we're doing pretty good so far."

As they returned to Macon, recharged and ready to face the challenges ahead, both Toby and Laura felt a renewed sense of purpose. The road they were traveling wasn't easy, but it was one they were building together—brick by brick, step by step.

Their lives were crossing paths in ways they had never imagined, and with every connection they forged, their bond grew stronger, their shared vision clearer.

18

A Shared Vision

———◄○►———

The rhythm of Toby and Laura's lives had settled into a steady beat—long days filled with work and study, balanced by evenings spent laughing and sharing dreams over takeout dinners. Yet, as the weeks passed, a quiet question lingered between them: *What comes next?*

It wasn't an easy question to answer, but both Toby and Laura knew it was one they couldn't avoid. Their paths had crossed and merged in ways they hadn't anticipated, and the love they shared had grown stronger with every step. Now, they found themselves standing at the threshold of the future, ready to take the next leap—together.

One Friday evening, as they sat across from each other at their favorite Italian restaurant, Toby leaned forward, his expression thoughtful.

"Have you ever thought about... what our future might look like?" he asked, his voice steady but curious.

Laura tilted her head, her fork resting on the edge of her plate. "You mean where we'll live? What we'll do? All of it?"

He nodded, his gaze searching hers. "Yeah. I mean, we've talked about some of it before, but I want to know what *you* see when you imagine it."

She smiled, her eyes shining with emotion. "I see us building something—something meaningful, something that lasts. Maybe starting small, with a place of our own. Then figuring out the rest as we go."

Her words settled over him like a warm blanket, filling him with a quiet certainty. "That sounds perfect."

The following weekend, Toby and Laura strolled through a quiet neighborhood on the outskirts of Macon, the autumn air crisp and refreshing. The houses lining the street were modest but charming, each with its own personality—front porches adorned with rocking chairs, gardens bursting with fall blooms, mailboxes painted in cheerful colors.

"This feels right," Laura said, her voice light but earnest. "Not too big, not too flashy—just home."

Toby nodded, his hand brushing hers as they walked. "I could see us here. Making it our own, little by little."

Her laughter rang out, bright and full of promise. "You really mean it, don't you?"

"I do," he said, his voice carrying a note of certainty. "And I think... when the time's right, we'll make it happen."

That night, as they sat side by side on the couch, a notebook open between them, Laura sketched out ideas for what their future home might look like—a space that blended comfort with character, practicality with warmth.

Toby added his own thoughts, describing a small garden in the backyard where they could grow fresh vegetables, a cozy reading nook bathed in sunlight, and a welcoming kitchen where they could experiment with recipes.

"This is exciting," Laura said, her voice bubbling with energy. "It's like we're creating a vision— not just for a place, but for our lives."

He smiled, his hand resting lightly on hers. "And it's a vision I can't wait to make real—with you."

As if on cue, a letter arrived from Reverend Tanner the following week, his handwritten words carrying the same steady wisdom Toby had always admired.

Toby, the letter began, *it brings me so much joy to hear about the life you're building with Laura. Watching you grow into the man you've become has been one of the greatest blessings of my years as pastor. Remember, the best foundations are built on love, faith, and commitment. Trustin these things, and you'll find that everything else will fall into place.*

Toby read the letter aloud to Laura that evening, her smile widening with every word.

"He always knows just what to say," she remarked, her voice soft.

"Yeah," Toby replied, his gaze steady. "And he's right—we've got everything we need to start building."

The road to the future stretched out before them, filled with possibilities they hadn't yet imagined. Toby and Laura knew there would be challenges along the way—moments of doubt and uncertainty—but they also knew they had the strength to face them together.

As they stood on the porch of their apartment that evening, the stars above them twinkling like tiny promises, Toby wrapped his arms around Laura and whispered, "Here's to our vision— whatever it becomes."

She leaned into him, her voice steady and filled with love. "Here's to us."

19

Rising Foundations

———◄◆►———

The acceptance letter from Emory University arrived on a rainy Thursday morning. Toby stared at the envelope for a moment, his heart pounding as he tore it open. The words

"Congratulations!" leapt off the page, and for a brief moment, the weight of the world lifted as excitement flooded in.

Laura was the first person he called, his voice trembling with a mixture of pride and disbelief.

"I got in," he said, barely able to contain his emotions.

Her gasp of joy was immediate. "Toby, that's incredible! I knew you could do it."

But with the good news came a new set of challenges—leaving Macon, starting over in Atlanta, and figuring out how their lives would fit together in a city neither of them fully knew.

The decision for Laura to transfer her medical studies to Emory and search for a job in Atlanta came naturally, though it wasn't without its hurdles. Together, they dove into the logistical maze of applications, apartment hunting, and budgeting for the next chapter of their journey.

"You're sure about this?" Toby asked one evening as they sifted through listings for apartments near Emory.

Laura looked at him, her gaze steady. "I've never been more sure of anything. We've come this far together—I'm not letting a little distance stop us now."

Her confidence bolstered his own, and soon they found a modest apartment a few blocks from campus—a space that was small but full of potential.

The move to Atlanta was a whirlwind, the city's bustling streets and towering skyline a stark contrast to the quieter pace of Macon. Their first days in the apartment were a blur of unpacking, navigating unfamiliar neighborhoods, and adjusting to the hum of a city that seemed to never sleep.

Laura quickly secured a job as an administrative assistant at a private medical practice in Midtown—an opportunity that allowed her to balance work with her transfer to Emory's medical program.

"It's not exactly where I saw myself starting," she admitted one night as they ate takeout on the floor of their still-unfurnished apartment.

"But it's a step forward," Toby replied, his voice filled with encouragement. "And that's what matters."

Toby's first day at Emory was a mix of nervous excitement and quiet determination. The campus buzzed with energy, its stately architecture and sprawling greenery a backdrop to the whirlwind of orientations and introductions.

Dr. Patel, his new advisor, was a sharp and insightful woman who quickly recognized Toby's potential.

"You've got a good head on your shoulders," she told him during their first meeting. "But this program is going to test you in ways you haven't been tested before. Are you ready for that?"

Toby met her gaze, his voice steady. "I am."

The coursework was intense, pushing him to new limits, but he found solace in the steady rhythm of late-night study sessions, his research internship, and the unwavering support of Laura.

Laura's days were equally demanding, split between the fast pace of the medical practice and her studies at Emory. Yet, despite their packed schedules, she and Toby made it a priority to carve out moments of connection—whether it was a quick coffee date between classes or a quiet evening watching the city lights from their balcony.

One evening, as they shared a simple dinner of sandwiches and soup, Laura looked at Toby with a thoughtful expression.

"Do you ever think about how far we've come?" she asked. "From Pitney to Macon to here... it feels like we've lived a lifetime already."

He smiled, reaching for her hand. "I think about it all the time. And I think we're just getting started."

As the weeks turned into months, Toby and Laura began to find their rhythm in Atlanta—a balance of ambition and love, of pursuing their individual dreams while building a shared future. The challenges they faced were daunting, but with each obstacle they overcame, they grew stronger, both as individuals and as a team.

Standing on the threshold of their new life, they knew the road ahead would be filled with unknowns. But they also knew they had each other—and that was enough to keep moving forward.

20

Foundations in Harmony

The move to Atlanta marked the beginning of a new chapter, one brimming with possibility and transformation. Toby and Laura found themselves surrounded by the bustling energy of a city that seemed to mirror their own ambition. Yet amidst the excitement, they clung to the simple things—the laughter they shared, the dreams they nurtured, and the quiet moments that reminded them why they had chosen this journey together.

Their little cottage in Emory Village became the heart of their new life. Its ivy-covered exterior and creaky wooden floors carried an old-world charm that spoke to them both, and though the space was small, it was filled with light, warmth, and the promise of everything to come.

As they unpacked their lives into this new home, each box felt like a step toward the future they had imagined. The front porch became a sanctuary for late-night talks, the kitchen a place of shared meals and laughter, and the cozy living room a haven where they could simply *be*.

Toby's acceptance into Emory's medical program was both a triumph and a challenge. The rigorous coursework tested his limits, the late nights in the library pushed his stamina, and the complexity of case studies often left him questioning his abilities.

But with every challenge came growth. His advisor, Dr. Patel, became a guiding force, offering wisdom that carried him through the most difficult moments.

"Toby," she said one evening after a particularly grueling lab session, "you have something rare—an ability to connect with people in a way that transcends knowledge. Never lose that. It's what makes a great physician."

Her words stayed with him as he navigated the demands of the program, a reminder that his journey wasn't about mastering science—it was about making a difference.

While Toby immersed himself in his studies, Laura found her footing in Atlanta. Her role at the Midtown medical practice introduced her to the fast-paced world of healthcare administration, where every day brought new challenges and opportunities to grow.

At the same time, she continued her medical studies at Emory, her determination driving her through long hours and heavy workloads. Though balancing work and school was far from easy, Laura approached it with the same grace and tenacity that had carried her through every step of her journey.

"I'm learning so much," she told Toby one night as they sat on their porch, the city lights twinkling in the distance. "Not just about medicine, but about myself. It's like... everything is starting to make sense."

He smiled at her, admiration shining in his eyes. "That's because you're incredible, Laura. You make everything look easy."

She laughed softly, her hand finding his. "And you make everything worth it."

Amid their busy schedules, Toby and Laura carved out time to dream—about the life they were building, the future they envisioned, and the foundation they wanted to lay for everything to come.

On quiet evenings, they sat at the dining table with notebooks and sketches, imagining a home where love and purpose could thrive. It wasn't just about walls and furniture—it was about creating a life that reflected their values, their journey, and their unwavering belief in each other.

"This is where it all starts," Toby said one evening, his voice steady as he looked at Laura. "Right here, with us."

She nodded, her smile soft but full of conviction. "And it's only going to grow from here."

As Toby and Laura stood on the porch of their cottage, the evening air filled with the hum of crickets and the faint rustle of leaves, they felt a quiet sense of fulfillment. Their journey had taken them from the small town of Pitney to the heart of Atlanta, through challenges that had tested their resolve and moments that had strengthened their love.

The road ahead was still full of uncertainties, but they faced it with confidence—knowing that together, they could build a life rooted in love, resilience, and hope.

As Toby wrapped an arm around Laura, pulling her close, he whispered, "Here's to everything we've built—and everything we'll build."

She smiled, leaning into him as her voice echoed his sentiment. "Here's to us."

21

Anatomy of a Dream

The first day of Toby's anatomy course at Emory was one he wouldn't soon forget. The atmosphere in the lab was somber yet reverent, the room filled with students who understood the gravity of what lay ahead. At the center of it all was the cadaver—a silent teacher whose lessons would shape their understanding of the human body in ways textbooks never could.

Dr. Patel stood at the front of the room; her voice steady as she addressed the class.

"What you're about to embark on is more than just a study of anatomy," she said. "It's a journey of respect, curiosity, and growth. Remember, this is not just science—it's humanity."

Over the course of the year, Toby's time in the anatomy lab became a defining part of his experience at Emory. The precision required for dissections, the intricate details of the human form, and the sheer complexity of the systems within it pushed him to new heights of focus and determination.

There were moments of awe—like the first time he traced the delicate network of nerves in the arm—and moments of frustration when a procedure didn't go as planned.

But through it all, Toby found himself growing—not just in knowledge, but in appreciation for the fragility and resilience of life.

One day, as he worked alongside Angela and another classmate, Samuel, Dr. Patel paused to observe their progress.

"This work demands patience and respect," she said, her tone both instructive and encouraging. "And you've shown both in abundance. Keep it up."

Toby often found himself reflecting on the lessons he learned in the lab. Sitting on the porch of the Emory Village cottage, he shared his thoughts with Laura one evening as the stars blinked into view above them.

"It's humbling," he admitted, his voice thoughtful. "Every time I think I've figured something out, I realize how much I still don't know."

Laura reached for his hand, her grip reassuring. "That's what makes you great, Toby. You're always willing to keep learning—to keep growing."

He smiled at her, the weight of the day lifting slightly as they sat in the quiet embrace of the evening.

In addition to his coursework, Toby began an internship at Emory University Hospital—a role that brought him face-to-face with the realities of patient care. Shadowing physicians during rounds, assisting with charting, and observing procedures became his new normal.

One particular day stood out in his memory—the first time he witnessed an emergency procedure to save a patient's life. The urgency, the precision, and the teamwork on display left him both awed and inspired.

Afterward, Dr. Bennett, who had transferred from Macon to join Emory's faculty, pulled Toby aside.

"Medicine isn't just about fixing what's broken," she said. "It's about understanding the whole person—their fears, their hopes, their story. Never lose sight of that."

Her words resonated deeply, shaping how Toby approached every patient encounter moving forward.

The demands of Emory tested Toby in ways he hadn't anticipated. The long hours, the emotional toll of patient care, and the constant drive for excellence left him exhausted at times.

But through it all, he found strength in the support of Laura. Her words of encouragement, her unwavering belief in him, and the quiet moments they shared reminded him why he had chosen this path.

"You're doing something amazing, Toby," she said one night as they sat at the dining table, her voice steady. "Even on the hardest days, you're making a difference."

Her faith in him became a light he carried through the darkest moments, fueling his determination to keep moving forward.

As the semester ended, Toby felt a deep sense of accomplishment—not just for what he had learned, but for how he had grown.

The experiences at Emory had challenged him, shaped him, and prepared him for the next steps on his journey.

Sitting on the porch of their cottage one evening, he turned to Laura with a thoughtful smile.

"I couldn't have done this without you," he said softly.

She smiled, her gaze steady and full of love. "You're not doing it without me, Toby. We're building this together."

22

Clinics

———◆◇◆———

The transition from classroom learning to clinical rotations marked a significant shift in Toby's journey through medical school. The sterile halls of Emory University Hospital became both his classroom and his proving ground, each patient interaction an opportunity to learn, grow, and connect on a deeper level.

"You're stepping into a new world now," Dr. Patel told him on his first day of rotations. "What you'll learn here can't be found in textbooks. It's about people—their stories, their resilience, and their trust in you. Don't take that for granted."

Toby's early days in rotations tested him in ways he hadn't expected. The long hours, the weight of responsibility, and the need to make split-second decisions left him exhausted yet exhilarated. Each department brought its own challenges—from the fast-paced chaos of the emergency room to the quiet intensity of pediatrics.

One particularly tough moment came during his internal medicine rotation when a patient he had been working with took a sudden turn for the worse. Despite the team's best efforts, they couldn't save her.

"It's not your fault," Dr. Patel said gently after the case. "Sometimes, even when we do everything right, it's not enough. The best thing you can do is carry what you've learned forward—and honor the trust they placed in you."

The experience left Toby shaken but also more determined than ever to give every patient his all.

Amid the trials, there were moments of triumph that reminded Toby why he had chosen this path. During his cardiology rotation, he assisted in a procedure that saved a patient's life—a moment that left him both awed and inspired.

"You have a steady hand and a calm mind," the attending physician said afterward. "That's rare,

Toby. You're going to make a great doctor."

The praise filled him with quiet pride, a validation of the countless hours he had poured into his studies and training.

Through it all, Laura remained Toby's anchor. Her own days were filled with the demands of her medical studies and work at the Midtown practice, yet she never hesitated to offer him encouragement when he needed it most.

One evening, as they sat on the couch surrounded by notes and laptops, Toby let out a long sigh.

"Some days, I feel like I'm barely keeping my head above water," he admitted.

Laura placed a comforting hand on his knee. "You're doing more than that, Toby—you're thriving. I see it in the way you talk about your patients, the way you light up when you learn something new. You're exactly where you're meant to be.

Her words were a balm to his weary spirit, a reminder that he wasn't navigating this journey alone.

One of the most profound lessons Toby learned during his rotations came from an elderly patient named Mr. Jenkins, who had been hospitalized for complications from diabetes.

Mr. Jenkins had a knack for storytelling, weaving tales of his youth with humor and wisdom that captivated everyone around him.

"You know, Doc," he said one afternoon as Toby checked his vitals, "life's not about getting everything right. It's about finding the good in what you've got—and holding onto it."

The words stayed with Toby long after Mr. Jenkins was discharged, shaping the way he approached not just his patients, but his own life.

As the year drew to a close, Toby and Laura celebrated a milestone together: passing their respective midterm evaluations with flying colors. The achievement felt like a testament to their hard work, resilience, and the strength of their partnership.

"This calls for a celebration," Laura said with a grin as they toasted with mugs of hot cocoa on their porch.

"To us," Toby replied, his voice filled with gratitude. "For everything we've overcome—and everything we've still got to conquer."

With each challenge and triumph, Toby grew not just as a medical student, but as a person. The lessons he learned at Emory—the resilience of his patients, the trust of his mentors, and the steadfast support of Laura—became the building blocks of the doctor he was becoming.

And as he looked toward the future, he knew one thing for certain: with Laura by his side, there was nothing he couldn't face.

23

Echoes in the Night

———◆○◆———

It was a night like any other—a quiet evening in the Emory Village cottage with Laura fast asleep beside him. The faint hum of the air conditioning was the only sound in the room, its steady rhythm lulling Toby into a light slumber.

But sometime in the middle of the night, he was jolted awake, his heart pounding and his breath coming in quick, shallow gasps. The darkness around him seemed to close in, and for a fleeting moment, he wasn't in his bedroom anymore. He was back in the cold, dim dormitory of the Industrial Home, the faint echo of footsteps reverberating down the corridor.

The vision came rushing back—a memory he had buried deep but never fully forgotten. It was the night he lay awake in his bunk, staring at the cracked ceiling above him, his thoughts heavy with fear and longing for home.

Down the corridor, the strained, shallow breaths of another boy filled the air—labored and uneven, each one a struggle. Toby remembered the muffled voices of the staff, their movements hurried yet somber.

By morning, the boy was gone. He had passed away quietly in the night; his absence felt like a void that permeated the entire dormitory.

Toby hadn't known him well, but he had seen the pain in his eyes—the exhaustion and defeat that seemed to seep into every corner of that place. The memory of that moment, of life slipping away so quietly and unnoticed, was something Toby carried with him long after he left the Industrial Home.

Sitting up in bed, Toby rubbed his hands over his face, trying to steady his racing thoughts. The memory felt as vivid now as it had on the night it happened, its weight pressing down on him with a familiar heaviness.

He turned to Laura, her peaceful face illuminated by the faint glow of moonlight filtering through the curtains. The urge to wake her was strong, but instead, he slipped quietly from the bed and made his way to the porch.

The cool night air wrapped around him as he sat on the porch steps, his gaze fixed on the stars above. Memories of the Industrial Home played on a loop in his mind—not just the boy's death, but the collective suffering and hopelessness that had defined so many of the boys' lives there.

Toby hadn't been able to save that boy, but the experience had planted a seed within him—a quiet yet unwavering determination to make a difference, to ensure that no one felt as abandoned and unseen as they had in that place.

Laura's soft voice broke through his thoughts as she stepped onto the porch, her robe wrapped snugly around her.

"Toby?" she said gently, her concern evident as she sat beside him. "What's wrong?"

He hesitated for a moment before sharing the memory, his voice steady but tinged with emotion.

"That boy..." he said finally, his words catching in his throat. "He didn't deserve to die like that— alone, scared. None of us deserved to be there."

Laura reached for his hand, her grip firm and grounding. "You can't change what happened, Toby. But you can carry it with you. And you can use it to shape what comes next—for you and for the people you want to help."

Her words brought a lump to his throat, a reminder of the strength he found in her unwavering belief in him.

As the night wore on, Toby found himself returning to a place of quiet resolve. The echoes of the Industrial Home might never leave him, but they didn't have to define him as they once did. Instead, they could serve as a guiding force—a reminder of why he had chosen this path and what he hoped to achieve.

"I want to make sure no one feels like that again," he said softly, his gaze still fixed on the stars.

Laura leaned against him, her head resting lightly on his shoulder. "You already are, Toby. Every patient you help, every life you touch—you're making a difference."

Her words settled over him like a warm blanket, filling him with a sense of peace he hadn't felt in years.

As Toby and Laura returned inside, the memory of the Industrial Home remained, but its weight felt lighter somehow transformed from a haunting echo into a source of strength.

Toby knew the road ahead would be filled with challenges, but the lessons he carried from his past would guide him forward, reminding him that even in the darkest moments, there was always a way to rise above.

24

The Heart of Medicine

———◄○►———

Toby's rotations in his final year at Emory were marked by intensity and discovery, each department offering unique insights into the world of medicine. From the fast-paced urgency of the surgical unit to the delicate care required in oncology, Toby found himself constantly challenged and inspired.

His favorite rotation, however, was in cardiology, a specialty that fascinated him with its combination of technical precision and human resilience.

"You've got a knack for this," Dr. Jensen, the attending cardiologist, said one afternoon as Toby assisted in a procedure to implant a pacemaker. "You're calm under pressure and meticulous in your work—two qualities that will serve you well in this field."

The praise filled Toby with pride, validating the countless hours he had spent refining his skills and deepening his understanding.

One of the most impactful moments of Toby's cardiology rotation came with a patient named Mrs. Ellison—a spirited woman in her seventies who had been admitted for complications related to heart disease.

From the moment Toby met her, he was struck by her resilience and sense of humor, even in the face of uncertainty.

"Don't let this old ticker fool you," she said with a wink as Toby checked her vitals. "It's got plenty of fight left."

Over the course of her treatment, Toby found himself drawn to Mrs. Ellison's optimism and strength. Their conversations ranged from her favorite books to her stories of traveling the world in her youth.

"You remind me of my grandson," she said one afternoon, her voice soft. "He's got that same look in his eye—like he's ready to take on the world."

Her words stayed with Toby long after she was discharged, reminding him of the impact a single patient could have on his journey.

Not every day was filled with success. There were moments when Toby found himself grappling with the weight of responsibility—patients whose conditions deteriorated despite his best efforts, long hours that left him physically and emotionally drained, and the constant pressure to meet the expectations of his mentors and peers.

One particularly difficult case involved a young man named Caleb who had suffered a heart attack. Despite the team's quick intervention, complications arose that led to long-term challenges for the patient.

"I feel like I failed him," Toby admitted to Dr. Jensen one evening as they reviewed Caleb's progress.

Dr. Jensen placed a reassuring hand on Toby's shoulder. "Failure isn't in trying and falling short. It's in not trying at all. You gave him a fighting chance, and that's more than most people ever get."

The words served as a reminder to Toby that medicine was as much about resilience as it was about skill—a balance he was learning to navigate with every patient he encountered.

Amid the challenges, Toby leaned heavily on Laura, whose unwavering support became his anchor through the storms of medical school. Her own days were filled with the demands of her medical studies and work at the practice in Midtown, yet she never hesitated to offer Toby the encouragement he needed to keep going.

"You're doing something incredible," she said one evening as they sat on the couch, her voice steady. "Even on the hardest days, you're making a difference in people's lives."

Her words filled Toby with a sense of calm, reminding him why he had chosen this path—and why he wanted her by his side every step of the way.

As Toby neared the end of his rotations, a quiet moment of clarity came during an overnight shift in the ER. The department was quiet for once, the usual chaos replaced by the soft hum of monitors and the occasional footsteps of nurses making rounds.

Sitting at a desk reviewing charts, Toby felt a sense of calm settle over him—a realization that despite the challenges, he was exactly where he was meant to be.

"This is it," he whispered to himself, the words steady and certain. "This is what I've been working for."

With his rotations complete and graduation on the horizon, Toby found himself reflecting on the journey that had brought him here. The lessons he had learned, the patients who had touched his life, and the strength he had found in Laura all combined to shape him into the doctor he was becoming.

Standing on the porch of their cottage one evening, Toby turned to Laura with a thoughtful smile.

"I couldn't have done this without you," he said softly.

She smiled, her gaze steady and full of love. "You're not doing it without me, Toby. We're building this together."

25

The Threshold of Change

———◄○►———

The day of Toby's graduation dawned clear and bright, the kind of spring morning that seemed to hum with possibility. For Toby, it was more than a ceremony—it was a culmination of every late-night study session, every moment of doubt, and every instance where he chose to keep moving forward. It was a day that marked not just the end of medical school but the beginning of his career as a doctor.

Standing in his room, dressed in his ceremonial gown, he took a deep breath and looked at himself in the mirror. The young man staring back at him wasn't just a student from Pitney trying to prove himself. He was someone who had overcome adversity, grown through experience, and embraced the calling he had worked tirelessly to fulfill.

Laura met Toby outside the auditorium, her smile radiant as she adjusted his cap with a tenderness that spoke volumes.

"You did it," she said, her voice steady but full of emotion. "All those sleepless nights, all those sacrifices—you made it."

Toby smiled, his hands finding hers. "We made it. I couldn't have done any of this without you."

The ceremony itself was a blur of applause, speeches, and the collective excitement of graduates stepping into their futures. When Toby's name was called, he crossed the stage with a confidence that reflected not just his hard work but the support of everyone who had believed in him.

That evening, Toby and Laura hosted a small gathering at their cottage to celebrate the milestone. Friends from Emory, mentors like Dr. Patel and Dr. Bennett, and even Angela joined them, the space filled with laughter, shared memories, and the warmth of camaraderie.

Dr. Patel raised her glass during the toast, her voice steady yet heartfelt.

"To Toby," she said, "who has shown us all the power of resilience, dedication, and heart. You've made us proud, and we know you're going to do remarkable things."

The applause that followed was genuine, each person in the room a testament to Toby's journey.

With graduation behind him, Toby turned his focus to the next chapter: residency. He had been accepted into the Internal Medicine program at Emory University Hospital—a role that promised both challenges and growth.

"Residency is going to push you harder than anything you've faced," Dr. Patel warned during their final meeting. "But it's also going to shape you into the physician you're meant to be. Trust yourself, Toby—you've got what it takes."

The first days of residency were grueling, filled with long hours, complex cases, and the unrelenting demands of patient care. But with every challenge came moments of triumph—like the first time Toby successfully managed a case on his own, earning praise from his attending physician.

"You handled that beautifully," the attending said, clapping Toby on the shoulder. "Keep it up— you're on the right track."

As Toby navigated the intensity of residency, Laura remained a constant source of encouragement. Her own days were busy with work and her medical studies, yet she always found time to be there for Toby—whether it was bringing him dinner during late-night shifts or simply listening as he shared the highs and lows of his day.

One evening, as they sat on their porch with mugs of tea in hand, Laura turned to Toby with a thoughtful smile.

"You're doing something incredible," she said softly. "Even when it's hard, even when it feels overwhelming—you're making a difference."

Her words brought a sense of calm to Toby, reminding him of the strength he found in their partnership.

As Toby settled into residency and embraced the challenges ahead, he found himself reflecting on the journey that had brought him to this point. The lessons from Pitney, the memories of the Industrial Home, the grow that Mercer and Emory—all of it had shaped him into the person he was becoming.

And with Laura by his side, he knew there was nothing they couldn't face.

26

Farewell in Pitney

---◄O►---

The call came late in the evening, its piercing ring cutting through the quiet of the Emory Village cottage. Toby answered instinctively, his voice steady but tired.

"Toby," Mama's voice broke through, trembling with grief. "It's your daddy... he's gone."

The weight of her words settled over him like a heavy fog, and for a moment, the world seemed to still. He clutched the phone tightly, his breath catching in his throat as the reality sank in.

"We'll be there," Toby said finally, his voice soft but resolute.

The drive back to Pitney was quiet, the familiar sights of the countryside passing by in a blur. Laura sat beside Toby, her hand resting on his, offering silent support.

When they arrived at the family home, Toby was struck by how unchanged it seemed—the same weathered porch, the same creaking screen door, the same scent of Mama's cooking lingering in the air. But inside, the absence of his father was palpable, a void that seemed to echo through the walls.

Mama greeted them at the door, her eyes red and puffy but filled with warmth as she embraced Toby tightly.

"He loved you so much," she whispered, her voice breaking.

"I know," Toby replied, his own tears threatening to spill. "I loved him too."

The wake was held in the small church where Toby had spent countless Sundays with his family. Friends and neighbors gathered, their voices hushed as they offered condolences and shared memories of the man who had been a pillar of strength for so many.

Robbie stood near the front; his usual mischievous grin replaced by a somber expression.

"He was proud of you, Tob," Robbie said, his voice steady but full of emotion. "Always said you were gonna change the world."

Toby nodded, his heart heavy but filled with gratitude for the love his father had shown him, even in the quietest moments.

After the wake, Toby found himself wandering the fields behind the house, the golden light of dusk casting a warm glow over the landscape. Laura joined him, her presence a comforting balm to his aching heart.

"This place," he said, his voice thoughtful. "It's where I learned everything—the good, the bad, and everything in between. Daddy taught me how to stand tall here, even when the world felt like it was falling apart."

Laura slipped her hand into his, her touch grounding him. "He'd be so proud of you, Toby. For everything you've done, for the person you've become."

He smiled faintly, the bittersweet sting of her words settling deep in his chest. "I just wish he could see it."

The funeral was a quiet affair, the sound of hymns filling the air as Toby stood beside Mama, his arm wrapped around her shoulders. The pastor's words were gentle, reflecting the life of a man who had been devoted to his family and his faith.

As the coffin was lowered into the ground, Toby felt a wave of emotions crash over him—grief, gratitude, and a quiet resolve to honor his father's legacy in everything he did.

That evening, as Toby and Laura sat on the porch of the family home, the stars above blinking softly in the night sky, Toby made a quiet promise.

"I'm going to keep making him proud," he said, his voice steady despite the tears that brimmed in his eyes. "Every day, in everything I do."

Laura placed a comforting hand on his shoulder, her own eyes shimmering with emotion. "You already are, Toby. You've been making him proud every step of the way."

When they returned to Atlanta, Toby carried the memory of his father with him—a guiding force that reminded him of where he came from and why he had chosen this path.

The lessons his father had taught him—the value of demanding work, the importance of family, and the strength to persevere—became the foundation on which Toby continued to build his dreams.

27

Forging Strength

———◦———

R esidency wasn't just a step forward for Toby—it was a cru-
cible that pushed him to his limits and tested the resolve
he had spent years building. The days were long, the demands
relentless, and the stakes higher than ever. But through it all, Toby
found himself growing in ways he hadn't imagined, each challenge
shaping him into the doctor he was meant to become.

One of Toby's most daunting experiences came during his first
rotation in critical care. The patients he encountered were often
balancing on the edge between life and death, their cases demanding a level of precision and compassion that left no room for error.

One evening, Toby was tasked with managing a patient who had
suffered a severe stroke. As he stood at the bedside reviewing vitals
and coordinating with the attending physician, he felt the weight
of responsibility settle heavily on his shoulders.

"You've got this," the attending reassured him, her tone steady. "Trust your instincts."

Though the case was fraught with challenges, Toby rose to the occasion, his calm demeanor and thorough approach earning the respect of his colleagues.

Amid the intensity, there were moments that reminded Toby why he had chosen this path. During his cardiology rotation, he successfully managed a particularly complex case involving a young woman with heart failure.

"Thank you," she said softly as he checked on her before discharge. "You gave me hope when I thought I had none."

Her words filled Toby with a sense of fulfillment that carried him through even the hardest days.

Not every case ended in success. The loss of patients—especially those he had come to know and care for—took an emotional toll that Toby hadn't fully prepared for.

One evening, after losing a patient to complications from a rare disease, Toby sat in the hospital break room, his hands trembling slightly as he tried to process the grief.

Laura found him there during a rare visit to bring him dinner, her presence a quiet comfort.

"You did everything you could," she said gently, her hand resting on his arm. "And that matters more than you know."

Her words brought a quiet reassurance, reminding Toby that even in loss, his efforts carried meaning.

Throughout his residency, Toby leaned heavily on the wisdom of his mentors. Dr. Patel, who had been a guiding force since his days as a medical student, continued to offer insights that shaped Toby's approach to patient care.

"Medicine is about more than healing the body," she told him during a late-night debrief. "It's about understanding the human spirit—their fears, their hopes, and their resilience. Remember that, Toby. It will make you not just a good doctor, but a great one."

Her words became a mantra for Toby, influencing the way he connected with patients and colleagues alike.

Despite the grueling demands of residency, Toby made a point to carve out moments of connection with Laura. Whether it was sharing a meal in the hospital cafeteria during her visit or taking a quiet walk-through Emory Village, their partnership remained a source of strength and grounding.

One evening, as they sat on the porch swing watching the city lights flicker in the distance, Toby turned to Laura with a thoughtful expression.

"You make me better," he said softly.

Laura smiled, her hand resting lightly on his knee. "And you make me proud, Toby. Every single day."

As Toby approached the midpoint of his residency, he found himself reflecting on the journey that had brought him here. The lessons from Emory, the challenges of patient care, and the unwavering support of Laura all combined to shape him into the physician he was becoming.

Though the road ahead was still full of uncertainties, Toby felt a quiet confidence in his ability to face them—knowing that with resilience, determination, and love, he could rise above anything.

28

Heartbeats of Opportunity

———◆◇◆———

It was during a routine cardiology rotation that Toby first encountered Dr. Nathan Greer, a seasoned cardiologist known for his sharp intellect and no-nonsense demeanor. Dr. Greer had a reputation for being tough but fair, his expectations high but always accompanied by an eye for talent.

The initial encounter between Toby and Dr. Greer was anything but smooth.

"Dr. Ashton," Greer said curtly, gesturing toward Toby as they reviewed the charts of a patient with acute heart failure, "why isn't this lab work updated?"

The unexpected confrontation left Toby momentarily flustered, but he quickly recovered, his calm demeanor returning as he explained.

"The updated results were delayed at the lab," Toby replied, his voice steady. "I've followed up, and they're expected within the hour. In the meantime, I've noted the prior trends and adjusted the treatment plan accordingly."

Greer studied him with a piercing gaze, his silence stretching just long enough to make Toby's pulse quicken.

"Fair response," Greer said finally, his tone neutral but carrying a hint of respect. "I hope you realize this isn't about treatment plans—it's about anticipating what comes next. You've got brains, Dr. Ashton, but I need to see if you've got the heart for this."

Over the next few weeks, Toby found himself working closely with Dr. Greer, whose rigorous approach to patient care pushed Toby to new levels of precision and foresight. The cases they encountered ranged from routine procedures to high-risk surgeries that demanded nothing short of excellence.

One case stood out—a young man named Marcus who had been admitted with a rare congenital heart defect. The complexity of Marcus's condition required a multidisciplinary approach, with Toby and Greer leading the charge.

"Toby," Greer said during a team meeting, his tone sharp but encouraging, "what's your analysis of Marcus's echocardiogram?"

Toby presented his findings with confidence, outlining a treatment plan that balanced both urgency and caution.

"It's bold," Greer remarked, nodding as he reviewed the plan. "But it's sound. You might have a future in this field yet."

The praise bolstered Toby's confidence, but it also reinforced the need to keep proving himself.

After weeks of intense collaboration, Dr. Greer approached Toby one evening in the hospital cafeteria, his expression unreadable.

"You've got talent, Ashton," Greer said without preamble, his tone steady. "More than I expected. I'm building a new team in the advanced cardiology unit—people who can think on their feet, adapt under pressure, and drive innovation. I want you on it." Toby's breath caught, the weight of the offer settling over him like a tidal wave.

"I... I don't know what to say," he admitted, his voice trembling slightly. "Say yes," Greer replied simply. "And show me what you can do."

Later that evening, Toby shared the news with Laura, his excitement bubbling over despite his exhaustion.

"Dr. Greer asked me to join his team," Toby said, his voice filled with disbelief and pride.

Laura's eyes widened, her smile brightening the room. "Toby, that's incredible! I knew he'd see how amazing you are."

"I'm not sure I'm ready for it," Toby confessed, his doubt creeping in.

Laura took his hands in hers, her gaze steady and reassuring. "You are ready, Toby. You've worked for this—earned it. And I'll be right here, cheering you on every step of the way."

Joining Dr. Greer's team marked a turning point in Toby's residency—a moment that pushed him to new heights and opened doors to opportunities he hadn't imagined. The challenges would be greater, the stakes higher, but Toby felt a quiet confidence in his ability to rise to the occasion.

With Laura by his side and his passion for cardiology driving him forward, Toby knew that the road ahead was filled with possibilities—each heartbeat a reminder of the impact he could make.

29

Mastering the Beat

———◦———

J oining Dr. Greer's advanced cardiology team was both an honor and a test for Toby—a chance to prove himself among some of the brightest minds in the field. The work was demanding, the hours grueling, and the expectations higher than ever. But for Toby, it was also an opportunity to push the boundaries of what he thought he was capable of.

Toby's first week on the team plunged him into the heart of complex cases that required split second decision-making and a deep understanding of cardiology. The morning case reviews were rigorous, with Dr. Greer questioning each team member's analysis and treatment plans.

"Toby," Greer said one morning, gesturing toward an angiogram displayed on the screen.

"What's your interpretation of the blockage in the left anterior descending artery?"

Toby stepped forward, his voice steady as he explained the findings and recommended an intervention.

Greer's sharp gaze lingered on him for a moment before he nodded. "Good. Now tell me what the backup plan is if that approach fails."

Though the question caught Toby off guard, he quickly outlined an alternative strategy, earning a rare but approving smile from Greer.

The fast pace of the unit taught Toby to think on his feet and trust his instincts. One particularly tense moment came during a late-night emergency where a patient's heart rhythm deteriorated rapidly.

"Toby, you're up," Greer said, stepping back as the team sprang into action.

With the weight of the moment pressing on him, Toby focused on stabilizing the patient, his hands steady and his mind clear as he worked through the procedure.

When the patient's condition improved, Greer clapped him on the back. "Not bad, Ashton," he said, his tone carrying a hint of pride. "You've got the nerves for this."

Amid the challenges, there were moments that reminded Toby why he had chosen this specialty. During a research project led by Greer, Toby explored innovative techniques for managing heart failure—a field that fascinated him with its potential to change lives.

"Stay curious," Greer advised as they analyzed the data. "The best doctors are the ones who never stop asking questions."

The project ignited Toby's passion for discovery, pushing him to dive deeper into the intricacies of cardiology.

Word of Toby's skill and dedication began to spread throughout the hospital. Patients spoke of his compassionate care, colleagues admired his ability to stay calm under pressure, and even the notoriously tough Greer began to rely on him for critical cases.

"You're starting to make a name for yourself," Laura remarked one evening as they sat on the porch, sharing a rare quiet moment.

Toby smiled, his gaze thoughtful. "I just want to make a difference. That's what this has always been about."

Laura reached for his hand, her touch grounding him. "And you are, Toby. More than you know."

The defining moment of Toby's time on Greer's team came during a groundbreaking procedure that pushed the boundaries of traditional cardiology. Toby played a key role, his precision and focus earning him accolades from both the team and the patient's family.

"That was exceptional," Greer said afterward, his praise rare but heartfelt. "You've got what it takes, Toby. Don't let up."

The words filled Toby with a quiet pride, a validation of the years of hard work and resilience that had brought him to this point.

As Toby continued to thrive on the team, he found himself dreaming of what lay ahead—not just in cardiology, but in his broader journey as a physician. The lessons he learned under Greer's mentorship, the challenges he overcame, and the victories he achieved became steppingstones toward the future he envisioned.

With Laura's unwavering support and his passion driving him forward, Toby knew the possibilities were endless—and that the best was yet to come.

30

Laura's Path

While Toby excelled on Dr. Greer's cardiology team, Laura was carving her own path in the world of medicine. Her work at the Midtown medical practice had grown from a temporary job to a role where she was trusted and respected, her talent for balancing administrative precision with compassionate care earning her the admiration of both her colleagues and the patients she served.

But it was her studies at Emory that challenged her in ways she hadn't anticipated, pushing her to the limits of her endurance and teaching her lessons that went beyond textbooks and lectures.

Laura's days began early and ended late, a whirlwind of classes, rotations, and shifts at the practice. It often felt like there weren't enough hours in the day, but Laura tackled each challenge with quiet determination, her vision of the future keeping her grounded.

One particularly hectic day saw Laura managing a scheduling crisis at the practice while preparing for a critical exam at Emory. Her supervisor, Ms. Gaines approached her with an apologetic smile.

"You've got a lot on your plate, Laura," she said gently. "Don't hesitate to let me know if it's too much."

Laura smiled; her exhaustion hidden behind her professional demeanor. "I can handle it," she replied. "It's all part of the journey."

During a clinical rotation in pediatrics, Laura found herself drawn to the energy and resilience of the young patients she worked with. One patient, a boy named Liam who was undergoing treatment for leukemia, left a particularly deep impression on her.

Despite the gravity of his illness, Liam faced each day with a smile and an endless supply of jokes that brightened the entire ward.

"You're going to be okay," Laura told him one afternoon as she reviewed his progress. "You've got more strength than most people I know."

"And you've got better bedside manners than most doctors," Liam quipped, his laughter filling the room.

The experience reminded Laura of why she had chosen medicine—to make a difference, even in the smallest of ways.

On nights when their schedules aligned, Laura and Toby would sit together on the porch, their conversations weaving between the triumphs and trials of their respective journeys.

"You've got this glow about you," Toby remarked one evening, his voice warm. "Even when you're exhausted, you're still inspiring."

Laura laughed softly, her hand resting lightly on his. "That's called being delirious. But honestly, Toby, I'm just trying to keep up with you."

"You're not keeping up," he replied, his tone serious. "You're leading the way."

Their shared moments of support and encouragement became a source of strength for both, a reminder that they were in this together, even as their paths diverged and converged.

Toward the end of her rotation, Laura received an offer to stay on at the Midtown practice as a resident after completing her studies—a milestone that filled her with pride and excitement.

"It's not the end goal," she told Toby that evening as the celebrated with takeout and laughter, "but it's a step in the right direction."

"And that's all that matters," Toby replied, raising his glass. "To you, Laura—the most incredible partner and future doctor I know."

Laura's path was one of perseverance and vision, a journey that reflected not just her ambition but the depth of her character and compassion. With each challenge she faced, she grew stronger, her resolve unwavering even in the face of uncertainty.

And as she looked toward the horizon, Laura knew that no matter where her journey led, she and Toby would continue to build a future defined by love, resilience, and the shared dream of making a difference.

31

A Promise Made

The idea of proposing to Laura had been on Toby's mind for weeks, the thought growing with each passing day until it became a quiet certainty. Laura was his anchor, his partner in every sense of the word, and he couldn't imagine a future without her by his side.

But this wasn't about asking a question—it was about creating a moment that reflected everything they had built together, from their humble beginnings in Pitney to the life they were forging in Atlanta. Toby wanted the proposal to feel as extraordinary as she was.

The plan came together one evening as Toby sat on their porch, the glow of the city lights inspiring an idea. He decided to take Laura back to the place where their journey began—the riverbank in Pitney, where they had shared countless dreams and promises as teenagers.

With the help of Robbie, who had always been Toby's partner in crime, he arranged for the spot to be decorated with fairy lights and candles, the setting as magical as the moment he envisioned.

On a crisp autumn evening, Toby and Laura returned to Pitney under the guise of visiting family. After dinner with Mama, Toby suggested they take a walk down to the riverbank, his heart pounding as he led Laura to the spot.

When they arrived, Laura gasped softly at the sight before her—the gentle glow of the lights casting a warm ambiance over the familiar setting.

"Toby," she said, her voice filled with wonder, "what is this?"

Toby turned to her, his hand slipping into his pocket to retrieve the small velvet box. Dropping to one knee, he looked up at Laura, his voice steady despite the emotions threatening to overwhelm him.

"Laura," he began, his heart full, "from the moment we met, you've been my best friend, my partner, my everything. You've stood by me through every challenge, celebrated every victory, and believed in me even when I didn't believe in myself. I can't imagine a life without you in it. Will you marry me?"

Tears filled Laura's eyes as she nodded, her smile radiant. "Yes, Toby. A thousand times, yes."

As Toby slipped the ring onto her finger and rose to embrace her, the world seemed to fall away, leaving only the quiet rhythm of the river and the love they shared.

The decision to hold the wedding at Laura's childhood church was an easy one. The small white chapel, nestled at the edge of town, held a special place in her heart, and Toby couldn't think of a more fitting setting for their union.

Over the next few months, they worked together to plan the ceremony, returning to the church on weekends to meet with the pastor and arrange every detail.

"Do you think your daddy would have liked this?" Laura asked one evening as they reviewed the guest list.

Toby smiled softly, his thoughts drifting to the man who had taught him the value of family and love. "I think he would have loved it, "he said. "And I think he'd be proud of us."

The morning of the wedding was filled with quiet anticipation, the chapel bustling with friends and family as they gathered to celebrate Toby and Laura's union. Mama fussed over Toby's tie as Robbie teased him about nervous grooms, while Laura's sisters helped her into her simple yet elegant gown.

When the music began and Laura walked down the aisle, Toby felt his breath catch. She was radiant, her smile brighter than the sunlight streaming through the chapel windows.

As they stood before the altar, the pastor's words resonated deeply, each vow a promise etched into their hearts.

"I now pronounce you husband and wife," the pastor said, his smile warm. "You may kiss the bride."

As Toby and Laura shared their first kiss as husband and wife, the room erupted into applause, their love a beacon that filled the chapel with joy and hope.

The reception, held in the churchyard under strings of twinkling lights, was a celebration of love and resilience. Toby and Laura danced beneath the stars, their laughter mingling with the sounds of music and the heartfelt toasts of their loved ones.

"This is just the beginning," Toby whispered as they swayed to the music, his gaze locked on Laura's.

She smiled; her voice filled with certainty. "And I can't wait to see what comes next."

32

Strength in Unity

———◆○◆———

The morning sunlight streamed through the curtains of their Emory Village cottage, casting a warm glow on the small space that Toby and Laura now called their shared home. Their wedding rings sparkled in the soft light, a tangible reminder of the promises they had made and the future they were building together.

Married life, though busy, brought a newfound sense of unity and purpose. The demands of their careers and studies were as intense as ever, but the knowledge that they were in it together gave them both a sense of balance and strength.

One evening, as Laura returned home from her shift at the Midtown medical practice, she found Toby already in the kitchen, his sleeves rolled up as he prepared dinner. The smell of garlic and rosemary filled the air, and a playlist of soft jazz played in the background.

"You're spoiling me," Laura teased, setting her bag on the counter and leaning in for a kiss.

"Just doing my part," Toby replied with a grin. "How was your day?"

They spent the evening swapping stories—Toby sharing the complexities of a particularly challenging case and Laura recounting her latest triumph at work. As they laughed over dessert, the weight of their responsibilities seemed to melt away, replaced by the warmth of their connection.

Their journey wasn't without its challenges. There were days when the exhaustion of their careers threatened to overwhelm them, moments of doubt when the weight of their ambitions felt too heavy.

One such moment came when Toby, in the middle of a particularly grueling week, found himself struggling to manage a difficult case that left him questioning his abilities.

"I don't know if I'm cut out for this," he admitted to Laura one night, his voice tinged with frustration.

Laura took his hand, her gaze steady and filled with unwavering support. "You are, Toby. You've proven it repeatedly. And even when it feels impossible, you're not doing it alone. We're a team, remember?"

Her words were a lifeline, pulling Toby out of the storm of self-doubt and reminding him of the strength they shared.

Amid the challenges, there were moments of pure joy that reminded them of the beauty of their journey. Weekend hikes through the trails near Atlanta, impromptu dance sessions in the living room, and quiet evenings spent dreaming of the future became the highlights of their busy lives.

One sunny afternoon, they visited a local farmer's market, their laughter echoing as they sampled fresh fruit and debated over which flowers to bring home.

"These," Laura declared, holding up a bouquet of sunflowers. "They're bright, cheerful, and impossible not to love."

"Just like you," Toby replied with a playful wink, earning a light-hearted shove and a smile that lit up her face.

As they settled into the rhythm of married life, Toby and Laura began to dream of what might come next—whether it was starting a family, pursuing new career milestones, or simply continuing to grow as individuals and as a couple.

One evening, as they sat on their porch swing watching the fireflies dance in the twilight, Toby turned to Laura with a thoughtful expression.

"Do you ever think about where we'll be in ten years?" he asked softly.

Laura smiled, her head resting on his shoulder. "All the time. And wherever we are, I know it'll be exactly where we're meant to be—as long as we're together."

With each passing day, Toby and Laura's bond grew stronger, their love deepening as they faced life's challenges side by side. They knew the road ahead wouldn't always be easy, but the strength they found in each other gave them the confidence to keep moving forward.

As they gazed out at the horizon, their hearts full of hope and determination, Toby and Laura knew that their journey was just beginning—and that the best was yet to come.

33

Shaping the Legacy

———◆○◆———

The morning rush at Emory University Hospital had become a familiar rhythm for Toby, the steady hum of activity energizing him as he prepared for another day on Dr. Greer's team. Each case brought its own challenges, but Toby approached them with the confidence and precision of a doctor who had found his purpose.

Laura, too, was thriving in her role at the Midtown medical practice, her leadership and expertise transforming her into a linchpin of the team. Though their days were busy and demanding, they both found joy in the work they were doing and the lives they were touching.

As Toby continued to excel in his position, Dr. Greer began entrusting him with more responsibility, including overseeing junior residents and leading case discussions.

"You're not just a team member anymore," Greer told him one afternoon after a particularly successful procedure. "You're a leader. Start acting like one."

Though the words carried weight, Toby embraced the challenge, mentoring younger doctors and sharing the knowledge he had gained through years of hard work and experience.

At the same time, Laura reached a pivotal moment in her career when she was promoted to Assistant Director of Operations at the Midtown practice. The new role allowed her to influence not only patient care but also the overall direction of the practice—a responsibility she took on with enthusiasm and determination.

"This is just the beginning," her supervisor, Ms. Gaines told her during their meeting. "You've got the vision and the drive to take this practice to the next level."

The promotion filled Laura with pride, a validation of the years she had spent balancing work, studies, and her partnership with Toby.

One quiet evening, as Toby and Laura sat on their porch swing with mugs of tea in hand, their conversation drifted to the future and the legacy they wanted to build.

"I've been thinking," Toby began, his voice thoughtful. "About what it means to leave something behind—not just in our careers, but in our lives."

Laura nodded, her gaze soft but curious. "You mean like a family? Or something bigger?"

"Both," Toby admitted, a smile tugging at the corners of his lips. "I want to make a difference, not just in the patients I treat but in the way we approach medicine—how we teach, how we care, how we innovate. And I want us to build something together, too."

Her smile widened, her hand finding his. "I think we're already doing that, Toby. Every day, with every step we take."

Inspired by their conversation, Toby, and Laura began brainstorming ways to combine their passions for medicine and community. The idea of starting a foundation—a program that provided access to healthcare for underserved populations—began to take shape, their shared vision driving their plans forward.

"We can do this," Laura said one evening as they sketched out ideas on a notepad. "We have the knowledge, the connections, and the drive. This could be our way of giving back."

Toby's heart swelled with pride and excitement, the thought of working alongside Laura on a project that combined their values and expertise filling him with purpose.

As Toby and Laura's careers continued to flourish, so did their dreams of building a legacy—one that reflected the resilience, love, and determination that had defined their journey from the very beginning.

Though the road ahead was still full of uncertainties, they faced it with confidence and hope, knowing that together, they could accomplish anything.

34

A Trial of Strength

———◦○◦———

It started as a dull ache in Laura's abdomen, the kind of discomfort that she brushed off as nothing more than stress or an overindulgent meal. But as the hours turned into days, the pain intensified, leaving her fatigued and struggling to focus.

"Toby," she said one evening as they sat on the couch, her voice strained, "I think something's wrong."

Her words immediately set off alarm bells in Toby's mind. He recognized the symptoms— radiating pain, nausea, and the persistent discomfort that seemed to worsen with time.

"We're going to the hospital," he said firmly, his tone leaving no room for argument.

At Emory University Hospital, Laura was quickly admitted and evaluated. Toby stayed by her side as the tests were run, his heart pounding with worry as the doctors worked to pinpoint the issue.

When the attending physician delivered the diagnosis—acute pancreatitis—Toby felt a mix of relief and concern. The condition, though serious, was treatable with proper care and monitoring.

"We'll keep a close eye on her," the doctor reassured. "She's in good hands."

During Laura's hospitalization, Toby barely left her side. He coordinated with her care team, reviewed her test results, and made sure she had everything she needed to stay comfortable.

"Toby," Laura said softly one evening as he adjusted her blanket, "you don't have to stay here all the time. You need to rest, too."

He shook his head, his eyes steady and resolute. "I'm not going anywhere, Laura. You've been there for me through everything—it's my turn to be here for you."

Her smile, though tired, carried a warmth that reminded Toby of the strength they shared.

There were moments during Laura's recovery that tested both—nights when the pain seemed unbearable, days when the uncertainty weighed heavily on their hearts.

"I feel so weak," Laura admitted one afternoon, her voice trembling as she fought back tears. "You're not weak," Toby replied, his voice firm but gentle. "You're one of the strongest people I know. And we're going to get through this—together."

His words became a mantra for both, a source of comfort and determination as Laura worked toward recovery.

After days of treatment and care, Laura's condition began to improve. Her pain subsided, her strength returned, and the sparkle in her eyes that Toby had always loved came back.

The attending physician met with them to discuss her progress, her tone optimistic.

"She's responding well to the treatment," the doctor said. "With continued care and some lifestyle adjustments, she should make a full recovery."

The relief Toby felt was palpable, and for the first time since Laura had been admitted, he allowed himself to breathe easily.

As Laura prepared to be discharged, Toby helped her into the car with a tenderness that spoke volumes.

"This was scary," Laura admitted as they drove home. "But it made me realize how lucky I am— to have you, to have this life we're building together."

Toby reached for her hand, his grip reassuring. "I'm the lucky one, Laura. And we're going to keep taking care of each other, no matter what."

Laura's battle with pancreatitis became a turning point in their partnership—a reminder of the resilience they shared and the strength they found in one another during life's toughest moments.

Together, they faced the road to recovery with hope and determination, knowing that no matter the challenge, their love was the foundation that would see them through.

35

Rising Above

———◄◦►———

The days following Laura's discharge from Emory University Hospital were a mix of quiet recovery and profound reflection. The ordeal of pancreatitis had left both Toby and Laura with a deeper appreciation for the fragility of life and the strength of their partnership.

Laura's focus shifted to regaining her health, her determination evident in every step she took toward recovery. Toby, ever by her side, became her strongest supporter, encouraging her on both the good days and the hard ones.

The weeks that followed were filled with doctor's appointments, dietary adjustments, and moments of progress that reminded Laura of the resilience she had always carried within her.

One sunny morning, as Toby prepared breakfast, Laura joined him in the kitchen, her steps slow but steady.

"You shouldn't be up yet," Toby said gently, his concern evident.

"I need to start moving," Laura replied with a faint smile. "I can't let this keep me down forever."

Her determination filled Toby with pride, a reminder of the strength that had drawn him to her from the very beginning.

As Laura regained her strength, she began to turn her attention back to her work at the Midtown medical practice and her plans for the foundation she and Toby had dreamed of creating.

"This isn't going to stop me," Laura said one evening as they reviewed their notes on the foundation. "If anything, it's given me even more motivation to make this happen."

Toby nodded, his admiration for Laura growing with each passing day. "We've got this," he said confidently. "Together, we can do anything."

When Laura returned to work, she was met with an outpouring of support from her colleagues, who admired her resilience and dedication. Her experiences during the illness gave her a new perspective on patient care, one that deepened her compassion and understanding.

"You've been through it," one of her colleagues remarked during a meeting. "And that makes you even more of an asset to this team."

The recognition filled Laura with gratitude and renewed energy, propelling her forward as she continued to make a difference in the lives of her patients.

For Toby, Laura's illness had been a stark reminder of the unpredictability of life and the importance of cherishing every moment. It also deepened his commitment to his work in cardiology, where he saw firsthand the impact that compassionate care could have on patients and their families.

One evening, as they sat on their porch watching the sunset, Toby turned to Laura with a thoughtful expression.

"This whole experience," he began, his voice steady, "it's made me realize how much more there is to do—not just in our work, but in how we live our lives."

Laura nodded; her gaze fixed on the horizon. "It's reminded me of what really matters—love, resilience, and the people who stand by us no matter what."

With Laura's health restored and their bond stronger than ever, Toby and Laura found themselves ready to take on the challenges and opportunities that lay ahead. They knew the road wouldn't always be easy, but their experiences had taught them that together, they could face anything.

As they planned their next steps—both personally and professionally—they carried with them a renewed sense of purpose and a shared vision for the future.

36

Breaking New Ground

———◄O►———

T he opportunity came unexpectedly, as most great challenges do. Toby was mid-shift in the advanced cardiology unit, reviewing patient charts, when Dr. Greer approached him with a file in hand.

"Dr. Ashton," Greer began, his tone sharp but measured, "we've got a new case—Mr. Colin Baxter, sixty-four, presenting with advanced aortic stenosis. Surgery is the best option, but his medical history complicates things."

Toby nodded, listening intently as Greer outlined the patient's condition. The narrowing of Mr. Baxter's aortic valve had progressed rapidly, putting immense strain on his heart and leaving him in critical need of intervention.

"This one's yours," Greer said, handing Toby the file. "You've got the skills, and I want to see what you can do. Let me know your plan by the end of the day."

The weight of the moment hit Toby immediately—this wasn't just another case. It was his chance to step into the spotlight, to prove himself not just as a member of the team but as a surgeon ready to innovate.

Toby dove into the case with focus and determination, reviewing every detail of Mr. Baxter's medical history, imaging, and lab results. The complexities of the case were undeniable—Mr. Baxter's prior heart surgery and underlying health conditions presented significant risks.

As Toby worked through potential approaches, an idea began to take shape—a minimally invasive valve replacement technique he had encountered during a recent research project but had never seen implemented in practice.

"It's bold," Toby admitted during the pre-operative meeting with Dr. Greer. "But I believe it reduces the risks associated with traditional open-heart surgery and improves recovery time."

Greer studied Toby for a moment, his expression unreadable. "If you're confident, I'll back you," he said finally. "But know this—if you're taking the lead, there's no room for error."

The operating room buzzed with quiet anticipation as Toby scrubbed in, his mind focused on the task ahead. The surgical team moved with practiced precision; their roles clearly defined as the procedure began.

With Greer observing from the side, Toby led the team through each step of the technique. His hands were steady, his voice calm as he guided the placement of the replacement valve through a small incision, carefully navigating the complexities of Mr. Baxter's anatomy.

The tension in the room was palpable as the final adjustments were made, the team holding their collective breath as Toby initiated the final test of the new valve's functionality.

As the monitor displayed a steady and strong heartbeat, a wave of relief and triumph washed over the room.

"It's working," one of the nurses said softly, a smile breaking through the tension.

Toby glanced at Greer, whose nod of approval carried more weight than any words could.

The procedure was a success, and Mr. Baxter's recovery exceeded expectations. Within days, he was sitting up in his hospital bed, his color returning and his strength improving with each passing day.

"Thank you," Mr. Baxter said when Toby visited him for a follow-up. "You gave me a second chance, and I'll never forget it."

Toby smiled, his humility shining through. "You did the hard part, Mr. Baxter—you fought through it. I'm only glad I could help."

The success of the procedure didn't go unnoticed. Greer made a point of highlighting Toby's innovation during the next team meeting, his praise both rare and meaningful.

"You've set a new standard, Ashton," Greer said. "Keep it up, and you'll go farther than you ever thought possible."

Toby's colleagues congratulated him, their respect for his skill and determination evident in their words and gestures.

That evening, as Toby recounted the experience to Laura on their porch, he found himself reflecting on the journey that had brought him to this point.

"It wasn't just me," he said softly. "It was all the people who believed in me—who pushed me to be better. I wouldn't be here without them."

Laura smiled, her hand resting lightly on his. "And now you're that person for so many others. You're doing exactly what you were meant to do."

The success of Mr. Baxter's case marked a turning point in Toby's career—a moment that proved not just his skill but his willingness to innovate and take risks for the sake of his patients. As he looked to the future, Toby felt a renewed sense of purpose and possibility, knowing that his journey was far from over.

37

The Ripple Effect

———◆◇◆———

The success of Mr. Baxter's case didn't just mark a milestone in Toby's career—it sparked a wave of curiosity and inspiration among his colleagues. The minimally invasive valve replacement technique he had implemented became the subject of discussions in team meetings, research papers, and even presentations at medical conferences.

Dr. Greer, ever pragmatic, wasted no time in encouraging Toby to take the lead on advancing the technique further.

"You've got something here," Greer told him during alate-night review of new cases. "And it's up to you to prove it's not just a one-off success. Expand it, refine it, make it the standard."

The challenge pushed Toby into uncharted territory, inspiring him to delve deeper into the intricacies of cardiology research and innovation.

At Greer's recommendation, Toby was invited to present the technique at a prestigious cardiology conference held in Atlanta. It was an opportunity unlike any Toby had experienced— a chance to share his work with some of the brightest minds in the field.

As Toby stood at the podium, his nerves threatened to overwhelm him. But as he looked out at the audience—Laura seated in the front row, her smile a beacon of support—he felt a calm confidence settle over him.

"This technique," he began, his voice steady, "is rooted in the belief that innovation and compassion go hand in hand. It's about improving outcomes while minimizing risks, and it has the potential to redefine how we approach valve replacement surgeries."

His presentation was met with applause and thoughtful questions from the attendees, their enthusiasm reflecting the impact of his work.

Back at Emory University Hospital, Toby began mentoring younger doctors who were eager to learn from his approach. His leadership style was collaborative, encouraging his mentees to think critically and push boundaries while always prioritizing patient care.

One of his mentees, Dr. Evelyn Carter quickly became a standout member of the team, her analytical mind, and steady hands earning Toby's respect.

"You've got potential," Toby told her after a successful procedure. "Keep working hard, and you'll go far in this field."

Evelyn's growth mirrored Toby's own journey, reminding him of the importance of passing on the lessons he had learned.

As Toby continued to refine the minimally invasive valve replacement technique, he collaborated with researchers and surgeons from around the country, each contributing their expertise to its development.

The work was demanding, often requiring long hours and intense focus, but Toby approached it with the same determination that had carried him through medical school and residency.

"We're just getting started," he remarked during a team meeting. "This is the beginning of something that could change lives—and I'm proud to be part of it."

At home, Laura remained Toby's anchor, offering him perspective and encouragement as he navigated this new chapter.

"You're doing something incredible," Laura said one evening as they sat on the porch, her voice filled with admiration. "And the best partis, you're staying true to who you are— compassionate, humble, and driven."

Her words grounded Toby, reminding him of the values that had always guided him.

Toby's groundbreaking work in cardiology wasn't about innovation—it was about creating a ripple effect that extended beyond the operating room, inspiring others to push boundaries and prioritize patient outcomes.

As he and Laura continued building their lives together, they found themselves dreaming not just of what they could achieve individually, but of the impact they could create collectively—a legacy defined by love, resilience, and the belief that every heartbeat carried the promise of something greater.

38

Expanding Horizons

---◄◆►---

The idea started as a passing thought—an inkling of something larger that kept tugging at Toby's mind during his quiet moments. His work in cardiology had flourished, and Laura's contributions to healthcare administration had left a visible mark on her practice. But as they talked through their dreams one evening, sipping tea on their porch, Toby couldn't shake the feeling that there was more they could do.

"What if we expanded?" he said suddenly, his voice carrying a spark of excitement.

Laura tilted her head, intrigued. "Expanded how?"

"Beyond Atlanta," Toby explained. "We've talked about creating a foundation—but what if it wasn't just a program? What if it became a movement, something that connected communities across the country?"

Laura's smile brightened as the idea took shape in her mind. "We could start by partnering with local clinics, hospitals, even universities.

Build networks, share resources, make healthcare accessible in places that need it most."

Over the weeks that followed, Toby and Laura began sketching out a plan to take their vision further. They reached out to colleagues, mentors, and friends, each conversation adding layers of depth and possibility to their concept.

"People want to help," Laura remarked during one of their brainstorming sessions. "They just need a platform—and that's what we can create."

Their passion was contagious, sparking enthusiasm from everyone they approached. Toby's reputation as an innovator and Laura's expertise in operations became the cornerstones of their burgeoning initiative.

The first step in their journey took them to Macon, a city that had always held significance for both. Partnering with local healthcare providers, they piloted a program that focused on preventative care, community education, and access to specialized treatments.

During the launch event, Toby spoke to a crowd of community members and healthcare professionals, his voice steady but filled with emotion.

"This isn't just about medicine," he said. "It's about creating connections, building trust, and ensuring that every person can live a healthy life. And it starts right here, with all of you."

The applause that followed was heartfelt, a testament to the impact they were already making.

The expansion brought challenges they hadn't anticipated—logistical hurdles, funding constraints, and the complexity of coordinating efforts across multiple organizations.

"This isn't easy," Toby admitted one evening as they reviewed their progress.

Laura nodded, her gaze steady. "But it's worth it. We're learning as we go, and that's what makes this meaningful."

Their resilience became their greatest asset, propelling them forward even when the road seemed uncertain.

As their initiative grew, Toby and Laura found themselves dreaming even bigger. They began envisioning a future where their work could span states, bridging gaps in healthcare and fostering collaboration among communities.

"We're planting seeds," Laura said during a late-night conversation. "And someday, those seeds are going to grow into something incredible."

Toby smiled, his heart full. "And we'll be there to see it happen—together."

With each step they took, Toby and Laura's horizons expanded, their vision becoming clearer and their impact more profound. They knew the journey wouldn't always be easy, but their partnership and shared determination gave them the strength to face whatever came their way.

As they looked to the future, they carried with them the belief that even the smallest steps could lead to something extraordinary—and that their work was just beginning.

39

Defining Moments

The case came to Toby's attention during morning rounds—a young woman named Emma, just twenty-six years old, admitted with severe cardiomyopathy. Her heart, weakened by an undiagnosed condition, struggled to sustain her, leaving her tethered to machines while awaiting a potential transplant.

The complexity of her case was undeniable. Not only was Emma's condition deteriorating rapidly, but her immune system presented unique challenges that made her compatibility with available donor hearts difficult.

As Dr. Greer outlined the situation during a team meeting; his eyes landed on Toby.

"This is as complex as it gets," Greer said. "And I want you to take point. We've pushed limits before—now it's time to see if we can redefine them."

Over the next several days, Toby and his team worked tirelessly to stabilize Emma, exploring every avenue to support her while she awaited a transplant. Toby's approach was methodical yet innovative, integrating new techniques and protocols he had studied but had yet to implement in practice.

Late one night, as Toby sat in the hospital's break room reviewing Emma's latest test results, Laura called to check in.

"How's she doing?" Laura asked, her voice soft but concerned.

"She's hanging on," Toby replied, his exhaustion evident. "But it's like we're running out of time.

I just... I need to find a way to give her a fighting chance."

Laura's words were both comforting and motivating. "If anyone can do it, Toby, it's you. You've faced impossible odds before—and you'll find a way through this, too."

Emma's case reached a critical juncture when Toby proposed an experimental approach—a device that could temporarily assist her heart while giving her body time to strengthen for a potential transplant.

It was a high-risk move, but after discussing the plan with Emma's family and receiving their consent, Toby moved forward with determination.

The surgery, which lasted hours, demanded every ounce of skill and focus Toby possessed. With Dr. Greer at his side, the team worked seamlessly to implement the device and stabilize Emma's condition.

As the final sutures were placed, the room erupted into quiet applause—a recognition of the success they had achieved against the odds.

Meanwhile, Laura's work with their foundation caught the attention of a major healthcare organization, which invited her to present their model at a national summit on community healthcare initiatives.

"This could change everything," Laura said one evening as she shared the news with Toby. "It's a chance to not only expand our reach but to inspire others to take action in their own communities."

Toby's pride was evident as he took her hands in his. "You've built something amazing, Laura.

And now you're going to show the world what's possible."

As days turned into weeks, Emma began to recover. The device had stabilized her condition, allowing her to gain strength while the search for a compatible donor heart continued.

"You saved my life," Emma told Toby one afternoon, her voice filled with emotion.

Toby shook his head, his humility shining through. "We're in this together, Emma. And we're going to keep fighting for you."

Emma's case became a defining moment in Toby's career, solidifying his reputation as a surgeon willing to push boundaries for the sake of his patients. At the same time, Laura's efforts with the foundation opened doors that promised to elevate their work to new heights.

Together, Toby and Laura faced the future with a renewed sense of purpose, knowing that their journey was about more than just success—it was about making a lasting impact on the world.

40

An Unexpected Gift

———◦———

The first hint that something was different came on an ordinary Thursday morning. Laura had been feeling unusually fatigued for days, brushing it off as the lingering effects of her illness combined with her demanding schedule. But when the nausea started—persistent and unrelenting—it became impossible to ignore.

"I'm sure it's just stress," she said to Toby one evening as they prepared dinner together.

Toby frowned, his concern evident. "Stress doesn't usually come with morning sickness, Laura. We should check."

Laura hesitated, the thought lingering in the air between them. They exchanged a look, a mixture of curiosity, hope, and nerves, before Toby made the decision for both.

"I'll go grab a test," he said, already reaching for his keys.

The result came quicker than either of them had anticipated. As Laura sat on the edge of their bed staring at the positive test in her hand, her emotions swirled in a kaleidoscope of disbelief, excitement, and anxiety.

"Toby," she said softly, her voice trembling as she looked up at him. "We're going to have a baby."

His reaction was instantaneous—a mixture of joy and incredulity as he wrapped her in a tight embrace. "Are you serious? Laura, this is... amazing."

Her laughter was laced with tears as she held onto him. "It's a little terrifying, too. Our lives are already so hectic. How are we going to handle this?"

Toby pulled back, his hands resting on her shoulders as he looked into her eyes. "Together. Like we always do."

The news of the pregnancy brought an immediate shift in their lives. Doctors' appointments, prenatal vitamins, and careful planning quickly became part of their routine, layered atop their already demanding schedules.

Laura, ever pragmatic, began researching everything she could about balancing pregnancy with her career, her notebook quickly filling with tips, schedules, and to-dos.

Toby, meanwhile, became even more protective of her, insisting on taking over household chores and sneaking nutritious snacks into her bag before she left for work.

"You don't have to baby me, you know," Laura teased one evening as he handed her a glass of water.

"I'm not babying you," Toby replied with a grin. "I'm just practicing for when the baby gets here."

Telling their families brought a mix of emotions, from Mama's tears of joy to Robbie's boisterous excitement.

"I always knew you two would end up with a little one," Mama said as she hugged Laura tightly.

"And I couldn't be happier for you both."

At the hospital, Dr. Greer's reaction was characteristically gruff but undeniably supportive.

"Congratulations, Ashton," he said with a nod. "But don't think for a second that I'm going to take it easy on you. Parenthood and surgery both require nerves of steel—consider this practice."

As the weeks turned into months, Toby and Laura began to prepare for their new roles as parents. Their evenings were spent assembling nursery furniture, debating baby names, and reading every parenting book they could get their hands on.

One night, as they sat together in the nursery, Laura leaned her head on Toby's shoulder, her voice filled with wonder.

"Can you believe this is happening?" she asked softly.

Toby smiled, his hand resting on her growing belly. "I can't wait to meet them, Laura. They're going to be the luckiest kid in the world to have you as their mom."

The unplanned pregnancy was more than just a surprise—it was a reminder of the unpredictability of life and the strength that Toby and Laura had found in each other. As they faced the challenges and joys of parenthood, they knew that their greatest adventure was just beginning.

41

Life in Motion

———◆◇◆———

L ife in the Ashton household had become a whirlwind of
activity, with Toby balancing high stakes surgeries and his
expanding role in cardiology, Laura dedicating herself to the foundation and her work at the medical practice, and the anticipation
of their growing family adding new layers of excitement and complexity.

Despite their hectic lives, Toby and Laura found moments of
quiet connection, their shared dreams propelling them forward
with a sense of purpose and unity.

Toby's work in cardiology continued to flourish, with Dr. Greer
entrusting him with more challenging cases and opportunities to
innovate. One particularly memorable case involved a patient with
a rare heart defect, requiring Toby to collaborate with a multidisciplinary team and implement innovative techniques.

"This is what you're meant for, Ashton," Greer said after the successful surgery. "Keep pushing boundaries—you're setting the standard for what's possible in this field."

Toby's contributions didn't go unnoticed, earning him recognition from colleagues and invitations to participate in national research initiatives.

Meanwhile, Laura's foundation had expanded its reach, with programs now operating in multiple states and partnerships forming with universities and healthcare organizations.

During a board meeting, Laura presented the foundation's latest achievements, her voice filled with pride and determination.

"We've impacted thousands of lives," she said, "but we're just getting started. Our vision is bigger than this, and I know we can achieve it."

Her leadership inspired the team, driving them to continue innovating and reaching underserved communities with compassion and care.

As Laura's pregnancy progressed, the rhythm of their lives adjusted to accommodate the changes. Toby attended every doctor's appointment, his medical expertise providing reassurance as they navigated each milestone.

During a particularly emotional ultrasound appointment, they heard the baby's heartbeat for the first time—a steady rhythm that filled them both with awe.

"That's our little one," Toby said softly, his hand resting on Laura's. "Strong and steady, just like you."

The months that followed brought moments of joy and challenges alike, with Laura balancing her work and the demands of pregnancy while Toby supported her every step of the way.

In the final weeks before the baby's arrival, Toby and Laura dedicated themselves to creating a warm and welcoming nursery. They spent evenings assembling furniture, hanging artwork, and debating over the perfect shade of paint for the walls.

"This is going to be their safe space," Laura said as she folded tiny onesies, her smile radiant.

"And they're going to be surrounded by so much love," Toby replied, his voice steady.

When the day finally came, it was as if time itself had paused. Laura went into labor in the early hours of the morning, and Toby stayed by her side through every contraction, his presence a source of strength and comfort.

"You're incredible," he said softly as she pushed through the pain. "You've got this, Laura."

The moment their child entered the world was one of overwhelming emotion—a mix of relief, joy, and awe as Toby and Laura held their baby for the first time.

"It's a boy," the nurse announced with a smile.

"He's perfect," Laura whispered, tears streaming down her face as she gazed at their son.

Toby's voice trembled as he leaned closer, his hand resting gently on the baby's tiny head. "Welcome to the world, little one. We've been waiting for you."

The arrival of their son brought a renewed sense of purpose and joy to Toby and Laura's lives. They embraced parenthood with the same resilience and determination that had carried them through every challenge, finding strength in the love they shared.

Though their lives were busier than ever, Toby and Laura knew that this new chapter was the start of something extraordinary filled with moments of growth, discovery, and boundless love.

42

Balancing New Beginnings

———◦———

Life with a newborn brought a rhythm unlike anything Toby and Laura had experienced—a symphony of sleepless nights, diaper changes, and tender moments that made every challenge worthwhile. Their son, Liam, had quickly become the center of their world, his tiny presence filling the cottage with love and laughter.

But balancing parenthood with two demanding careers was no small feat. For Toby and Laura, every day became a delicate dance of priorities, responsibilities, and moments of connection.

Toby took to fatherhood with the same determination he brought to his work. Late-night feedings became his specialty, giving Laura the chance to rest whenever possible.

One night, as Toby rocked Liam in his arms, singing softly to soothe him, Laura watched from the doorway with a smile.

"You're a natural," she said, her voice filled with admiration.

Toby looked up at her, his gaze warm. "I think I've got the best teacher," he replied.

Their partnership, already strong, deepened even further as they navigated the joys and challenges of parenting together.

At Emory, Toby's role in cardiology continued to expand, with new cases pushing the boundaries of his expertise. Balancing his demanding schedule with his responsibilities at home required careful planning—and the occasional sacrifice of sleep.

"Toby," Dr. Greer said during a case review one afternoon, "I don't know how you're managing all this. But keep it up—you're doing excellent work."

Meanwhile, Laura's foundation saw significant growth, with new initiatives reaching underserved communities across the country. Her team relied heavily on her leadership, which meant she had to find creative ways to juggle work and family life.

Despite their packed schedules, Toby and Laura made a point to carve out moments of connection—whether it was sharing a quick meal during Liam's nap or stealing quiet evenings on the porch after he fell asleep.

"Do you ever feel like we're just barely keeping up?" Laura asked one evening, her voice thoughtful.

Toby smiled, wrapping an arm around her shoulders. "Sometimes. But I think it's the good kind of chaos—the kind that means we're building something amazing."

As Liam grew, his milestones became the highlight of Toby and Laura's days. His first smile, his first laugh, and his first attempts at rolling over were met with cheers and laughter that filled the cottage.

One sunny afternoon, Toby and Laura watched as Liam reached for a toy with determination, his tiny fingers finally grasping it.

"He's got your persistence," Laura said with a laugh.

"And your charm," Toby replied, his grin matching hers.

As Toby and Laura settled into their new rhythm, they began dreaming of what the future might hold—for their careers, their foundation, and their family.

Sitting on the porch one evening, Liam asleep in Toby's arms, Laura turned to him with a thoughtful expression.

"What do you think comes next?" she asked softly.

Toby smiled, his gaze steady. "Whatever it is, I know we'll face it together."

With each passing day, Toby and Laura found themselves growing—not just as individuals, but as a family. The challenges they faced only strengthened their bond, reminding them that the beauty of their journey lay in the moments they shared.

43

Ambitions and Heartbeats

---◆○◆---

In the months following Liam's birth, Toby, and Laura found themselves navigating an intricate balancing act. Parenthood had brought new joys and challenges to their lives, while their careers and the foundation continued to demand their focus and determination.

The rhythm of their days was a symphony of diaper changes, board meetings, surgeries, and late-night feedings, yet through it all, they managed to find moments of connection and growth.

At Emory, Toby's role in cardiology reached new heights as he began leading clinical trials for innovative heart treatments and procedures. His groundbreaking techniques had earned him recognition across the field, and the demand for his expertise only grew.

One trial focused on a new biocompatible device designed to assist heart function without invasive surgery. Toby worked closely with researchers and engineers, pushing the boundaries of what was possible.

"You're creating solutions that could save countless lives," Dr. Greer remarked during a meeting. "Keep this momentum going, Siler—you're changing the game."

The validation fueled Toby's determination, reminding him of why he had pursued medicine in the first place.

Meanwhile, Laura continued to elevate the foundation's impact, her leadership inspiring new partnerships and initiatives. One program focused on maternal and child healthcare in underserved communities—a cause close to her heart after experiencing the challenges of pregnancy and motherhood firsthand.

"We're not just providing care," Laura said during a presentation to potential donors. "We're creating opportunities and hope for families who deserve every chance to thrive."

Her passion resonated deeply, resulting in a surge of support that allowed the foundation to expand its reach.

At home, Liam's growth brought both joy and exhaustion. As he began crawling and babbling, Toby and Laura found themselves chasing after their son with equal parts amusement and awe.

One evening, as Liam giggled uncontrollably while Toby tickled his feet, Laura captured the moment on her phone, her laughter filling the room.

"Pure joy," Laura said, smiling as she reviewed the video.

"And pure chaos," Toby replied with a grin.

Their shared moments as a family became the glue that held their hectic lives together, reminding them of the beauty in the simplest things.

Not everything came easily, though. Toby encountered a setback when a clinical trial faced unexpected delays due to funding issues. The challenges weighed heavily on him, but Laura's encouragement reminded him to persevere.

"You've done harder things," Laura said one night as they sat on the porch. "This is just another hurdle—and you'll overcome it like you always do."

Her words grounded Toby, renewing his sense of purpose and determination to push forward.

As Liam approached his first birthday, Toby, and Laura began dreaming of what their next chapter might hold—both as parents and as professionals.

One evening, as they watched Liam play with his favorite toy, Toby turned to Laura with a thoughtful expression.

"Do you ever think about what kind of world we're building for him?" he asked softly.

Laura nodded, her gaze steady. "All the time. And I think we're building something amazing— not just for Liam, but for everyone whose lives we've touched."

With each passing day, Toby, and Laura's journey continued to unfold, filled with ambition, love, and the quiet resilience that defined their partnership.

Though the road ahead was sure to bring new challenges, they faced it with confidence— knowing that together, they could turn every heartbeat into a moment of possibility.

44

Building Bridges

The ripple effects of Toby and Laura's work had begun to spread farther than they could have imagined. Their foundation, now a recognized force for change in healthcare, had become a beacon of hope for underserved communities. Meanwhile, Toby's reputation as a pioneer in cardiology continued to grow, solidifying his role as a leader in the field.

Yet amidst the accolades and progress, their focus remained steadfast: connecting with people, lifting others up, and creating a world where no one was left behind.

Laura's leadership of the foundation took a bold turn when she launched a mentorship program for aspiring healthcare professionals from underrepresented backgrounds.

"I want this to be more than just a support system," Laura explained during a team meeting. "I want it to be a launchpad for the next generation of changemakers."

Her vision led to partnerships with universities, clinics, and community organizations, creating pathways for students and young professionals to gain hands-on experience and build meaningful careers in healthcare.

During the program's first networking event, Laura watched as participants connected with mentors and shared their aspirations. One young woman approached her with tears in her eyes.

"Thank you," the woman said. "This program is giving me a chance I never thought I'd have."

Laura's heart swelled with pride and determination, knowing that their work was making a tangible difference.

At Emory, Toby had begun teaching surgical techniques to residents, his classroom a blend of theory, innovation, and hands-on learning.

One day, as he demonstrated an innovative approach to valve repair, a resident raised her hand. "Dr.

Siler, how did you learn to think creatively like this?"

Toby smiled, his tone thoughtful. "By being willing to fail. Every great idea starts with a risk— and every risk is worth it if it means we can save lives."

His mentorship became a source of inspiration for his students, many of whom credited Toby with shaping their careers and perspectives on medicine.

At home, life with Liam continued to be a source of joy and grounding for Toby and Laura. Their son's laughter filled the cottage, his energy a reminder of the simple beauty in everyday moments.

One evening, as they played together in the yard, Toby paused to watch Laura lift Liam into the air, her smile radiant as their son giggled uncontrollably.

"He's our greatest adventure," Toby said softly, his heart full.

Laura glanced at him, her expression matching his. "And we're just getting started."

The foundation reached a new milestone when it was invited to present at a global healthcare summit in Geneva. The opportunity was a testament to Laura's leadership and the collective efforts of their team.

"This is our chance to show the world what's possible," Laura said as she prepared for the presentation.

Toby, ever supportive, offered his encouragement. "You've already changed so many lives,

Laura. Now it's time to show everyone what we've built together."

The presentation was met with resounding applause, securing partnerships that promised to propel their work to an even greater scale.

As they reflected on their journey, Toby and Laura felt a deep sense of gratitude for everything they had built together—their family, their careers, and the bridges they had created to connect with others.

Sitting on the porch one evening, Toby turned to Laura with a smile. "Do you ever think about where this will all lead?"

Laura nodded, her voice steady. "I don't know exactly where, but I know it's going to be extraordinary—because we're building it together."

With every step they took, Toby and Laura's legacy grew, their impact rippling out to touch lives near and far. The road ahead was sure to bring new challenges and opportunities, but their bond, vision, and unwavering commitment to each other gave them the strength to keep moving forward.

45

Legacy in Action

———◆◇◆———

The foundation Toby and Laura had built over the years had grown into more than just an organization—it was a movement. Its programs now reached across the country, touching lives in ways they could never have imagined when they first started brainstorming ideas on their porch.

Meanwhile, Toby's innovative work in cardiology had inspired a new wave of treatments and protocols, cementing his reputation as both a pioneer and a compassionate physician.

During a visit to one of the foundation's community clinics in rural Alabama, Toby and Laura were met with heartfelt gratitude from the residents.

An older man, whose family had benefited from the clinic's resources, approached them with tears in his eyes. "You've saved not just lives, but hope," he said, shaking their hands firmly. "We'll never forget what you've done for us."

The moment was humbling, a reminder of why they had taken on this journey in the first place.

At Emory, Toby had become a mentor to countless residents and fellows, his teaching a blend of technical expertise and human connection. One of his mentees, Dr. Evelyn Carter had blossomed under his guidance, taking on challenging cases with the same determination that Toby recognized in himself.

"You've got what it takes," Toby told Evelyn after a complex surgery they'd performed together.

"And you're going to achieve things I can only dream of."

The pride in his voice reflected not just his confidence in her, but his belief in the importance of cultivating the next generation of doctors.

Laura's work with the foundation brought her to Washington, D.C ., where she was invited to speak before Congress about the importance of equitable healthcare. Standing before the assembled representatives, Laura shared stories of the people they'd helped, her passion evident in every word.

"This isn't just about healthcare," she said, her voice steady. "It's about dignity, about giving every person the chance to live a healthy, fulfilling life. And we have the power to make that happen."

Her speech earned a standing ovation and opened doors for new partnerships and funding opportunities, further elevating the foundation's mission.

Back home, Liam had begun toddling around the cottage, his curiosity and energy filling every corner of their lives. Watching their son grow became a source of endless joy, grounding Toby and Laura amidst the demands of their work.

One evening, as they sat on the floor playing with Liam, Toby turned to Laura with a smile. "He's going to be our greatest legacy," he said softly.

Laura nodded, her hand resting lightly on Toby's. "And he's going to know that anything is possible with love and determination."

To celebrate the foundation's tenth anniversary, Toby and Laura hosted a gala in Atlanta, bringing together friends, colleagues, and supporters who had been part of their journey.

As Laura addressed the crowd, her voice filled with gratitude and vision, Toby stood beside her, his pride unmistakable.

"This isn't just our success," Laura said, gesturing to the audience. "It's all of yours. Together, we're building a future that's brighter and more compassionate than we ever thought possible."

As they reflected on the journey that had brought them here, Toby and Laura felt a deep sense of fulfillment—not just for what they had achieved, but for the lives they had touched and the dreams they continued to chase.

With Liam by their side and their vision expanding beyond anything they had imagined, they knew that their story was far from over. The best, they realized, was yet to come.

46

Horizons Unfolding

———◄◦►———

Time had given Toby and Laura a sense of clarity—a realization that their journey was not just about accomplishing milestones but about continuing to evolve, both as individuals and as a family. The impact of their work was felt everywhere, yet their focus remained steadfast: creating meaningful connections and leaving a legacy rooted in compassion.

At Emory, Toby's career reached a pivotal moment when he was offered the opportunity to colead a national initiative focused on advancing treatments for congenital heart defects. The role demanded not only his expertise but also his leadership in fostering collaboration among surgeons, researchers, and institutions.

"This is a big step," Dr. Greer told him during their meeting. "You've proven yourself here, but now it's time to take your work to the next level—and I have no doubt you'll rise to the occasion."

Toby's decision to accept the role was met with excitement, though it came with the challenge of balancing his responsibilities at Emory with his new commitments on the national stage.

Meanwhile, Laura's foundation continued to grow, with innovative programs launching across multiple states. One initiative focused on training community health workers, empowering them to provide education and care in underserved areas.

During the launch event for the program, Laura's voice carried strength and vision as she addressed the audience.

"Change begins with people—and with the resources and opportunities to support them, there's no limit to what they can achieve," she said.

Her leadership inspired others to join the cause, further propelling the foundation's reach and impact.

At home, Liam was thriving—his curiosity and energy bringing joy to Toby and Laura's busiest days.

One evening, as Toby helped Liam build a tower with blocks, Laura watched with a smile, capturing the moment in her memory.

"You're building something great there," Laura teased, her laughter filling the room.

"And you're building something even greater with him," Toby replied, his grin matching hers.

The joy of parenting became their grounding force, reminding them of the beauty in the simplest moments.

The balance between work and family life wasn't always easy. Toby and Laura faced moments of exhaustion and doubt, particularly when the demands of their careers seemed overwhelming.

But in those moments, they leaned on each other, their partnership a source of strength and resilience.

"We're doing this together," Toby said one night as they sat on the porch, their hands intertwined. "And I wouldn't want it any other way."

As Toby and Laura continued building their lives and their legacy, they found themselves dreaming of what might come next—whether it was expanding their foundation internationally, writing a book about their journey, or simply finding more time to enjoy their family.

One evening, as they gazed out at the stars, Laura turned to Toby with a thoughtful expression.

"I think the best part about all of this," she said softly, "is knowing that no matter what comes next, we'll face it together."

Toby smiled, his heart full. "And I wouldn't want it any other way."

Their lives were a mosaic of ambition, love, and resilience—a testament to the power of partnership and the belief that every step forward brought them closer to something extraordinary.

47

The Commencement Speech

———◦———

The invitation to speak at Mercer University's commencement ceremony stirred something deep within Toby—a sense of gratitude and reflection. Standing at the podium in the same university where he had once begun his transformative journey, Toby prepared to deliver words that would inspire and encourage the next generation of graduates.

Toby adjusted the microphone and looked out over the sea of faces, each one brimming with anticipation and possibility.

"Good afternoon, graduates, faculty, and honored guests. It's an incredible honor to stand before you today, especially here at Mercer—a place that shaped not only my career but also the person I've become."

He paused, letting the moment settle before continuing.

"When I first arrived at Mercer, I was a young man carrying dreams that felt both too big and too distant. I had faced challenges that sometimes made me doubt if I'd see them come true. But what

I found here was a community—a network of people who believed in me, who challenged me, and who helped me rise to meet those dreams. Today, I want to share a bit of that journey with you, and I hope it will remind you of the power of resilience, connection, and vision."

Toby's tone softened as he drew on memories of his time at the Industrial Home in Pitney.

"Just down the street from this very campus, there stands—or I should say, used to stand—the Industrial Home, now abandoned and overgrown. For those of you who don't know its history, it was a place where boys were sent when society didn't know what to do with them. I was one of those boys.

The nights were long, the days were hard, and the dreams we carried often felt impossible. I remember lying awake one night, hearing the labored breaths of a boy who passed away alone in the corridor—a moment that's stayed with me ever since. It reminded me of how fragile life is, but also of how much hope and possibility we can bring to others when we refuse to give upon them.

Today, the Industrial Home is silent, its windows shattered and its walls crumbling. But I see it not as a symbol of defeat, but of transformation—of the power we must rise above, to rebuild, and to create futures that are brighter than what came before. And that's a power each of you holds as you step into your own journeys."

Toby smiled, his voice lifting as he began to recount the people who had carried him through.

"My story is not one of individual achievement, but of collective belief. I stand here today because of the mentors who taught me not just medicine but compassion—like Dr. Patel, who told me that healing is not just a science but an art of connecting with the human spirit.

I'm here because of Laura, my wife and partner, who has been my unwavering anchor and the greatest inspiration in my life. Together, we've built not just careers, but a family and a foundation that are about creating opportunities and hope for others.

And I'm here because of my community—the friends, professors, and colleagues who saw potential in me and refused to let me stop believing in myself. Their trust in me became the fuel for everything I've accomplished, and I'll carry it with me always."

Toby's voice grew steady and confident as he spoke about the road ahead.

"As you walk across this stage today and step into the next chapter of your lives, I urge you to dream boldly, to embrace the challenges that come your way, and to remember that every obstacle is an opportunity for growth.

The world is waiting for your ideas, your innovation, and your compassion. But it's also waiting for your connection—to one another, to the communities you will serve, and to the collective future you have the power to shape.

Whether you're building bridges in medicine, engineering, education, or the arts, remember that the legacy you leave behind is not in the accolades you achieve but in the lives you touch along the way. And in that spirit, I challenge you to ask yourselves: How can I make the world brighter for those who come after me?"

Toby took a moment to let the weight of his words settle.

"Graduates, Mercer University has prepared you well for the path ahead, but what lies beyond today is up to you. My hope is that you will go forward with courage, compassion, and the belief that anything is possible. As you carry your dreams out into the world, know that you are not alone—and that the greatest success is found in lifting others up with you."

He smiled; his voice filled with pride as he concluded.

"Congratulations, Class. You are the future, and the future is bright. Thank you."

The applause that followed was thunderous, the graduates and their families moved by Toby's heartfelt words. As he stepped away from the podium, Toby felt a sense of fulfillment and connection, knowing that his journey had come full circle—and that he had passed on the torch to the next generation of dreamers.

As Toby descended from the stage and the graduates began mingling with their families, his eyes were drawn to a familiar figure seated near the back—Reverend Tanner.

The sight of Tanner brought a rush of memories from Toby's time in Pitney—the kind words, the quiet prayers, and the unwavering belief that Tanner had shown him during some of the darkest days of his life.

As Toby approached Tanner, his steps steady but charged with emotion, Tanner rose to meet him, his smile warm and welcoming.

"Toby Ashton," Tanner said softly, extending his arms. "I always knew you'd find your way."

The embrace that followed was filled with years of unspoken gratitude and shared history; their connection rooted in moments that had shaped Toby into the man he was today.

They moved to a quieter corner of the auditorium, the noise of the celebration fading into the background as they sat down to talk.

"Seeing you up there," Tanner began, his voice thoughtful, "reminded me of the boy who used to sit in the back pew of my church, head bowed and heart heavy. You carried so much back then, Toby—and look at what you've done with it."

Toby's eyes glimmered with emotion as he nodded. "I wouldn't be here without you, Reverend Tanner. The way you believed in me when no one else did—it gave me hope when I didn't think there was any left."

Tanner smiled, his gaze steady. "You always had that spark, Toby. I just helped fan the flame."

They shared stories of the Industrial Home, recalling the resilience of the boys who had lived there and the quiet victories that Tanner had witnessed over the years.

"I went back there recently," Toby admitted, his tone reflective. "It's overgrown now, silent—but it feels like a place that's waiting for redemption."

Tanner nodded, his eyes distant but thoughtful. "Its redemption is in the lives of those who left it behind—and in the futures they've built. You, Toby, are one of its greatest redemptions."

Their conversation shifted to the present and the future, with Toby sharing his vision for the foundation and the impact he and Laura hoped to continue making.

"You're carrying your blessings forward," Tanner remarked. "And that's the greatest gift we can give—to take what we've been given and use it to uplift others."

Toby felt a quiet sense of resolve as he listened to Tanner's words, the weight of his journey and the hopes he carried becoming even clearer.

As they stood to part ways, Tanner placed a hand on Toby's shoulder, his voice filled with warmth and certainty.

"Keep going, Toby," he said. "Your path is one of purpose, and the world needs people like you to light the way."

Toby smiled, his gratitude overflowing as he embraced Tanner one last time. "Thank you—for everything."

Walking away, Toby felt a renewed sense of determination, his steps steady as he rejoined the celebration. Reverend Tanner's presence had been a reminder of the power of belief, connection, and the quiet acts of kindness that could change a life.

48

The Bonds We Build

———◀◆▶———

The days following Toby's speech at Mercer were filled with quiet reflection. Walking back onto that campus, recalling the overgrown Industrial Home, and embracing Reverend Tanner, had stirred something deep within him—a renewed sense of purpose and gratitude for the bonds that had carried him forward.

It reminded him that no journey, no matter how ambitious, is walked alone.

At Emory, Toby's mentorship of young doctors continued to flourish. His mentees admired not just his surgical expertise but his ability to connect on a human level. One resident, Dr. Brandon Yu came to Toby after a particularly difficult loss of a patient during surgery.

"I keep thinking there's something I could have done differently," Brandon admitted, his voice heavy with self-doubt.

Toby placed a reassuring hand on his shoulder. "We all feel that way, Brandon. Every loss stays with us—it's what keeps us human. But what matters is how you use that experience to grow, to keep doing your best for the next patient who walks through that door."

The conversation stayed with Brandon, who later thanked Toby for helping him find clarity and resilience in moments of doubt.

Laura's work with the foundation brought her back to Pitney for a new initiative focused on rural maternal healthcare. During her visit, she reconnected with Angela, her childhood friend who now worked as a nurse at the local clinic.

"It feels like everything's come full circle," Angela remarked as they toured the clinic together. "Who would've thought that two kids from Pitney would end up here, doing this?"

Laura smiled, her heart full. "It's amazing how our paths have brought us back to what really matters—helping the people who shaped us."

Their friendship deepened as they collaborated on the program, a reminder of the enduring connections that had supported Laura along the way.

At home, Liam's boundless energy continued to bring joy to Toby and Laura's lives. One sunny afternoon, they hosted a small family gathering at their cottage, with Mama, Robbie, and Laura's sisters joining them for a day of laughter, food, and memories.

As Liam toddled around the yard chasing bubbles, Mama pulled Toby aside, her eyes glistening with emotion.

"I'm so proud of you, Toby," she said softly. "You've come so far, and you've done it with kindness and strength."

Her words stayed with Toby, a testament to the power of the family bonds that had shaped him.

One evening, as Toby and Laura sat together on their porch, watching the stars twinkle above the trees, they found themselves reflecting on their journey.

"It's humbling," Toby said, his voice thoughtful. "How much we owe to the people who believed in us—Reverend Tanner, Dr. Patel, Mama, Robbie, Angela, Dr. Greer. They all played a part in getting us here."

Laura nodded, her hand resting lightly on his. "And now it's our turn to be that for others—for Liam, for the people we're helping through the foundation, for the students and doctors you're mentoring."

Toby smiled, his heart full. "It's a good legacy, isn't it?"

Laura's gaze softened. "It's the best legacy."

As Toby and Laura continued to build their lives and their impact, they were reminded daily of the bonds that sustained them—the friendships, mentorships, and family connections that gave their journey depth and meaning.

And as they looked to the future, they knew that the bonds they were building now would carry their dreams forward, creating a ripple effect that would touch generations to come.

49

A Higher Calling

———◄◦►———

The proposal arrived in a carefully worded email—an invitation for Toby and Laura's foundation to partner with global organizations to launch healthcare initiatives in underserved international communities. It was an opportunity unlike any they had encountered before, one that challenged them to think beyond the borders they had come to know.

"This could be life-changing," Laura said, her voice tinged with excitement as she read the email aloud to Toby one evening. "But it's also a huge leap for us."

Toby leaned forward, his eyes scanning the details. "It's a leap worth taking," he said confidently. "If we can do this, we can reach people who need care the most—and make a difference on an even greater scale."

The months that followed were a whirlwind of planning and collaboration. Laura worked tirelessly with her team to develop strategies for implementing programs in regions with limited resources, while Toby connected with international healthcare providers to discuss training and research opportunities.

Their first initiative focused on maternal and child healthcare in sub-Saharan Africa, combining medical services with educational outreach to empower communities.

"This isn't just about providing care," Laura explained during a meeting with the foundation's board. "It's about creating sustainable solutions—equipping people with the tools and knowledge to improve their own health and well-being."

Her passion inspired the team, igniting enthusiasm for the ambitious project.

Expanding internationally brought its share of challenges, from navigating cultural differences to addressing logistical hurdles. Toby and Laura quickly learned the importance of adaptability, relying on local leaders and experts to guide their approach.

During a meeting with community representatives, Toby listened intently as they shared their concerns and ideas.

"Your insight is invaluable," Toby said, his voice steady. "This is your community, and we want to make sure we're supporting it in a way that aligns with your needs."

The collaborative effort strengthened their bond with the communities they served, ensuring the initiatives were both effective and respectful.

As part of the expansion, Toby launched a mentorship program for young doctors and nurses in the partnering regions. His workshops focused on innovative techniques, patient-centered care, and the importance of resilience in the face of adversity.

During one workshop, a nurse approached Toby with gratitude.

"Dr. Siler," she said, her voice earnest, "your mentorship is giving us hope—showing us that even the toughest challenges can be overcome with compassion and determination."

The words resonated deeply, reminding Toby of the impact they were making, one connection at a time.

At home, Toby and Laura embraced moments of quiet reflection as they balanced the demands of the expansion with their family life. Liam, now a curious toddler, had started asking questions about the work his parents were doing.

"Where's Mommy going?" Liam asked one evening as Laura packed for a trip.

"She's going to help people who need doctors and medicine," Toby explained gently, lifting Liam into his arms. "Just like Daddy does."

Liam nodded thoughtfully, his innocent curiosity bringing a smile to both his parents' faces.

"He's already thinking about the world beyond himself," Laura said later, her voice filled with pride. "I hope he grows up knowing that he can make a difference, too."

Their first international initiative launched successfully, with clinics providing care and education to thousands of people. The impact was palpable, the gratitude and hope of the communities fueling Toby and Laura's resolve to continue pushing boundaries.

Standing outside one of the clinics, Toby turned to Laura with a thoughtful expression.

"Do you think this is what we were meant to do?" he asked softly.

Laura smiled, her hand resting lightly on his. "I think it's only the beginning."

The expansion marked a turning point in Toby and Laura's journey, opening doors to possibilities they had only dreamed of. With every step forward, they carried with them the belief that their work could create a ripple effect—transforming lives, communities, and futures across the globe.

50

A Legacy Rooted in Hope

---◆◆◇◆◆---

The years that followed their international expansion brought challenges and triumphs in equal measure. Toby and Laura's foundation became a model for transformative healthcare and education programs, but the road was never without obstacles.

Through it all, their belief in the power of connection remained unwavering. They knew that every clinic they launched, every conversation they had, and every life they touched were steps toward building a legacy of hope.

During one of their visits to Southeast Asia, Toby and Laura found themselves immersed in a small village nestled among the rice paddies. The foundation's new initiative focused on providing mobile health services to remote areas, with Toby leading a training program for local healthcare providers.

As he demonstrated an innovative emergency cardiac technique, Toby noticed the bright curiosity of one young nurse, Priya, whose questions reflected her eagerness to learn.

"You've got a gift, Priya," Toby said after the session, his voice encouraging. "Keep honing your skills—you have the potential to make an incredible difference here."

Priya's gratitude and determination reminded Toby of his own early days in medicine, igniting a sense of fulfillment and purpose.

Back in the States, Laura led a symposium that brought together leaders from healthcare, education, and community development. Her keynote speech outlined the foundation's vision for creating sustainable healthcare systems that empowered local leaders to take charge.

"This isn't just about fixing problems," Laura said, her voice steady. "It's about creating opportunities—about helping communities stand on their own and thrive in ways we never thought possible."

The attendees, inspired by her passion and clarity, pledged their support to expand the foundation's reach even further.

Not every step forward came easily. The global programs faced logistical issues that sometimes threatened their progress—equipment delays, funding shortages, and even skepticism from local governments.

During one particularly tense meeting with regional authorities, Laura remained calm and resolute.

"We're here to collaborate, not impose," she said. "We want to build something together— something that aligns with your goals and strengthens your community."

Her sincerity broke through the tension, paving the way for productive discussions and mutual trust.

One evening, as Toby and Laura sat together in a field overlooking the village they had been working in, the sunset painting the sky in hues of gold and orange, they found themselves reflecting on the journey they had taken.

"Do you ever wonder how we got here?" Toby asked softly, his gaze fixed on the horizon.

Laura smiled, her hand resting lightly on his. "Every day. And I think it's because we never stopped believing—in ourselves, in each other, and in the people we serve."

Toby's heart swelled with gratitude and love, their partnership a source of strength and inspiration.

Back home, Liam had grown into an inquisitive child who often asked questions about the world his parents were helping to shape.

During a bedtime story one night, Liam turned to Toby with wide eyes. "Do the people you help get to smile, Daddy?"

Toby smiled, his voice warm. "They do, Liam. And every smile means we're doing something good—something that makes the world a better place."

Laura, listening from the doorway, felt her heart fill with pride. Liam was already showing signs of the compassion and curiosity that defined his parents' journey.

As Toby and Laura continued to expand their work and deepen their impact, they carried with them the lessons they had learned along the way—that the greatest success is found in lifting others up and that hope can transform even the most challenging circumstances.

Their legacy was more than just programs and initiatives—it was the lives they had touched, the bonds they had built, and the hope they had inspired in communities around the world.

51

Bridging Continents

―――――◆◇◆―――――

The invitation came from a hospital in Nairobi, Kenya—a renowned medical center seeking to expand its capabilities in advanced cardiology. They had heard of Toby's groundbreaking techniques and were eager for him to share his expertise with their physicians.

"It's an incredible opportunity," Toby said as he discussed the trip with Laura one evening. "Not just to teach, but to learn—about how medicine is practiced here, and about the people who make it happen."

Laura smiled, her encouragement evident. "You're going to make a real difference, Toby. And you'll carry their stories with you, just like you always do."

Toby arrived in Nairobi with a sense of awe, the bustling city alive with energy and warmth. The hospital's staff greeted him warmly, their pride in their work evident as they showed him around the facility.

"This is more than just a hospital," Dr. Njeri, the chief cardiologist, explained as they walked through the wards. "It's a lifeline for our community—a place where people come not just for treatment, but for hope."

Toby nodded, his respect for the hospital and its mission growing with every word.

Over the next week, Toby led intensive training sessions with the hospital's physicians, focusing on the minimally invasive techniques that had revolutionized his work back home.

During one session, he demonstrated the delicate placement of a transcatheter valve, his hands steady and his explanations clear. The physicians watched intently, their curiosity and determination driving them to absorb every detail.

"This technique reduces risk and recovery time," Toby explained. "But it's not just about the procedure—it's about the patient. Always remember that you're treating a person, not just a heart."

The advice resonated deeply, sparking discussions about how they could adapt the techniques to their patients' unique needs.

Toby quickly discovered that the training was a two-way street. The physicians shared their own approaches to patient care, highlighting methods that had been shaped by the challenges and resilience of their community.

One afternoon, Dr. Njeri shared a case study involving a patient who had traveled hundreds of kilometers to reach the hospital, her determination to seek care inspiring the entire staff.

"She reminds us why we do what we do," Njeri said. "And I hope her strength inspires you as much as it inspires us."

Toby nodded, moved by the story. "It's stories like hers that remind us of the humanity in our work—and why it's worth every effort."

Outside of the hospital, Toby spent time connecting with the local community, visiting schools and clinics to learn more about the challenges they faced and the resilience they embodied.

One evening, he attended a gathering of healthcare workers under the open sky, their laughter and stories filling the air as they shared experiences and hopes for the future.

"These are the moments that stay with you," Toby remarked to Njeri. "The connections, the people—they're what make all of this meaningful."

As Toby's time in Nairobi ended, the physicians and staff expressed their gratitude, presenting him with a small token of appreciation—a beautifully carved wooden heart symbolizing their connection.

"You've given us more than just techniques," Njeri said during the farewell gathering. "You've given us inspiration—and the belief that we can push boundaries to provide better care."

Toby felt a quiet sense of pride and humility, knowing that the experience had been as transformative for him as it had been for them.

As he boarded the plane home, Toby carried with him not just the stories and lessons from Nairobi but a renewed sense of purpose. The trip had reminded him of the universal thread that ties us together—the desire to heal, to connect, and to create a better world for all.

52

Threads of Humanity

———◆◇◆———

From bustling cities to remote villages, Toby and Laura's work with their foundation took them to places they had only dreamed of. Each journey brought new challenges and opportunities, unveiling the shared humanity that tied their mission together.

Their dedication was unwavering, rooted not just in their expertise but in their belief that every life mattered—and that every thread of humanity was worth nurturing.

One of their latest initiatives brought Toby and Laura to a village nestled deep in the Amazon rainforest, where access to healthcare was limited and the need was urgent.

As they arrived at the community center—a modest building surrounded by towering trees— village leaders greeted them, whose warm smiles and heartfelt gratitude immediately set the tone for their visit.

"You've come a long way to help us," said Isabela, the village nurse. "And we are grateful for your presence."

Toby nodded, his humility shining through. "We're here to listen, to learn, and to share—and to work together to create solutions that make a difference."

Toby's focus during the visit was on training local healthcare providers, equipping them with skills to manage cardiovascular emergencies in areas where resources were scarce.

Through hands-on demonstrations, he taught techniques for diagnosing and stabilizing patients, emphasizing adaptability and creative problem-solving.

"Sometimes, the tools we need aren't available," Toby explained. "But that doesn't mean we stop trying. It means we find another way."

His words resonated deeply, inspiring the providers to think critically and innovate within their constraints.

Meanwhile, Laura worked with the village leaders to establish a healthcare education program tailored to the community's needs. She focused on building trust and fostering collaboration, ensuring the program reflected their unique challenges and strengths.

"This isn't just about implementing a plan," Laura said during one meeting. "It's about creating something sustainable—something that empowers you to take ownership and thrive."

Her approach garnered respect and enthusiasm, forging partnerships that promised lasting impact.

As their time in the village unfolded, Toby and Laura discovered moments that reminded them why they had chosen this path.

One evening, while sharing stories with the community under a star-filled sky, Toby was approached by an elderly man named Luis.

"My heart has slowed me down for years," Luis said quietly. "But your visit gives me hope—not just for myself, but for the young ones who will carry this community forward."

Toby's voice softened as he replied. "Hope is the strongest medicine there is. And you've reminded me of that tonight."

Back home, Liam eagerly awaited his parents' return, his curiosity about their work growing with each trip.

"What do the people look like where you went?" Liam asked as Toby showed him pictures from the rainforest.

"They look like us," Toby said, his tone thoughtful. "They smile, they laugh, they work hard—and they want the same things we do: health, happiness, and a future for their families."

Laura joined them, her voice filled with warmth. "And they helped remind us how connected we all are."

With each journey, Toby and Laura found themselves weaving new threads into the tapestry of their lives—threads of resilience, connection, and humanity that bound their work and their family together.

Their foundation wasn't about programs and initiatives—it was about honoring the strength of the people they served and carrying that strength forward into every step of their journey.

53

Coming Home

———◄●►———

The invitation came with a handwritten note from the principal—a warm message that expressed admiration for Toby's accomplishments and the hope that he would share his wisdom with the graduating class.

When Toby stepped into the halls of Pitney High School on the day of the ceremony, the air was thick with memories. The scuffed linoleum floors, the faded banners on the walls, the hum of students' laughter—it all transported him back to his own days as a lanky teenager, quietly carrying dreams that felt far out of reach.

Before the ceremony began, Toby was ushered into the faculty lounge, where several of his former teachers had gathered to greet him. Some had retired but returned for the occasion; others were still teaching, their smiles a mix of warmth and curiosity as they welcomed him back.

"Mrs. Wilkes," Toby said with a smile, recognizing his old English teacher. "You haven't changed a bit."

Her laugh was gentle, tinged with nostalgia. "Well, I don't run up and down the stairs quite like I used to, but I still remember your essays—the ones that showed me you had something special in you."

Mr. Harris, his chemistry teacher, shook Toby's hand firmly. "Didn't I tell you that science was the way forward?" he said with a wink.

Toby's gratitude overflowed as he exchanged memories and laughter with the teachers who had seen his potential even during the tough times.

As Toby stood at the podium before the graduating class, the auditorium quieted, the anticipation palpable. He adjusted the microphone, his gaze sweeping over the students, families, and teachers who filled the space.

"Good afternoon, graduates, families, and faculty," Toby began, his voice steady but touched with emotion. "It's an incredible honor to be here today, in a place that holds so many memories and so much significance in my life.

When I walked through these halls as a student, I wasn't sure where life would take me. I carried doubts, fears, and dreams that often felt impossible. But what I found here—in these classrooms, in the encouragement of my teachers, and in the friendships I built—was hope.

And today, I want to share with you the lessons that hope has taught me."

Toby spoke of his time at Pitney High, weaving in stories of the teachers who had shaped him, the classmates who had challenged him, and the moments that had pushed him to strive for more.

"I remember sitting in Mrs. Wilkes's class, learning how words could connect people and spark change. I remember Mr. Harris teaching me that curiosity is the foundation of progress. And I remember all the quiet conversations, the kind words, and the belief they had in me—even when I struggled to see it myself."

He paused, letting the weight of his words settle.

"What I've learned is that success isn't about doing it alone. It's about the people who stand beside you, who lift you up, and who remind you that you are capable of more than you ever imagined."

Turning his focus to the graduating class, Toby offered words of hope and challenge.

"As you step into the next chapter of your lives, I urge you to dream boldly, to embrace the struggles that come your way, and to lean on the people who believe in you. Know that your path will be unique, and it will be filled with moments that test your resilience and spark your growth.

But in those moments, remember that this place—this community—has given you a foundation. And the bonds you've built here will carry you forward, just as they carried me."

As Toby closed his speech, the applause thundered through the auditorium, the energy and emotion filling every corner of the room. He stepped away from the podium, his heart full as he joined the principal and faculty to greet the graduates.

Later, as the ceremony wound down, Toby found himself back in the lounge, sharing quiet moments with his former teachers.

Mrs. Wilkes's voice softened as she spoke. "It's good to see you've found your path, Toby. We always knew you would—sometimes it just takes time to find your way."

Toby nodded; his voice steady but filled with emotion. "You all gave me the courage to start— and I'll carry that with me always."

The conversations lingered, rich with memories and gratitude, as Toby reflected on the journey that had brought him back to where it all began.

As Toby walked out of Pitney High School that evening, the warm glow of the sunset stretching across the parking lot, he felt the threads of connection and hope that had carried him through his life. And with each step, he knew that the legacy he was building wasn't just for himself—it was for the people who had believed in him, and for the countless lives he hoped to touch in return.

54

A Moment by the Creek

A fter months of travel, work, and relentless schedules, the decision to take a few days off felt like a gift. Toby and Laura packed up the car, Liam tucked safely in his car seat and drove to spend time with family. Laura's parents welcomed them with open arms, and Toby's mama and brother, Robbie, joined soon after.

Their days were filled with laughter and warmth—meals shared around the table, Liam chasing fireflies in the yard, and the simple joy of reconnecting with the people who mattered most.

One crisp morning, Toby leaned over to Laura as they sipped coffee on the porch.

"Want to go for a walk?" he asked, his tone light but thoughtful. "I've been meaning to take you to a spot that's always been special to me."

Laura smiled; her curiosity piqued. "I'd love that."

With Liam staying behind under the watchful eyes of his grandparents, Toby and Laura set off, the quiet countryside enveloping them as they made their way toward Sinkhole creek.

When they reached the creek, Toby slowed his steps, taking in the familiar scene—the gentle trickle of water over smooth stones, the sunlight filtering through the canopy of trees.

"This is it," he said softly, gesturing to the spot where the bank curved into a small, shady nook. "This is where I used to come when things felt too heavy. It was my escape, my place to think and dream."

Laura glanced at him, her expression tender. "It's beautiful, Toby. I can see why it meant so much to you."

They settled onto the grass, the sound of the creek weaving its way into their conversation.

Toby ran a hand over the weathered bark of a nearby tree; his voice tinged with emotion as he began to share his memories.

"When I was a kid, I used to sit right here and skip stones, trying to make sense of everything. The Industrial Home, my dad, the weight of not knowing what the future held—it all felt a little lighter when I was here."

He paused; his gaze fixed on the water. "I remember thinking that if I could just hold on—if I could just keep believing—then maybe, just maybe, things would get better. And somehow, they did."

Laura reached for his hand, her touch grounding him. "You've come so far, Toby. And everything you've been through—it's what's made you the person you are today. Strong, kind, and resilient."

They sat in companionable silence for a while, the creek's melody filling the spaces between their thoughts. Toby skipped a stone across the water, smiling as it danced across the surface before sinking.

"Do you ever think about what Liam will grow up to dream about?" Toby asked suddenly, his tone introspective.

Laura's smile softened. "I hope he dreams big—just like his dad. And I hope he knows that no matter what, we'll always be here to believe in him."

Toby's heart swelled with gratitude and love, their shared vision for the future deepening his connection to Laura and their family.

As they made their way back to the house, hand in hand, Toby felt a sense of peace he hadn't experienced in a long time. The creek had served its purpose once again—not as an escape, but as a reminder of where he'd come from and how far he'd traveled.

When they stepped onto the porch, Liam greeted them with an excited giggle, running toward them with open arms.

"There's our little dreamer," Toby said, scooping Liam up and spinning him around as Laura laughed.

The day unfolded in the warmth of family, their bonds strengthened by the shared memories and the hope that carried them forward.

55

A Gathering of Minds

———◄○►———

T he idea of hosting a global summit for their foundation had started as a passing thought—a dream of uniting the changemakers, innovators, and leaders who had joined their cause over the years. But as the foundation grew, the dream began to take shape, evolving into a plan that would bring voices from around the world together in one place.

"This summit is more than just an event," Laura said during one of the planning meetings. "It's our chance to spark collaboration, to celebrate what we've achieved, and to pave the way for even greater impact."

Toby nodded, his gaze steady. "It's about sharing ideas and inspiring action—and showing people what's possible when we work together."

The months leading up to the summit were a whirlwind of activity, with Toby and Laura working closely with their team to coordinate planning, secure speakers, and craft an agenda that reflected the foundation's mission.

The summit was set to take place in Geneva, a city known for its international diplomacy and innovation. The venue—a grand hall overlooking Lake Geneva—embodied the spirit of connection and possibility that Toby and Laura hoped to foster.

"This is going to be incredible," said Angela, who had joined the foundation's leadership team as the head of community outreach. "The world is going to see what we've built—and where we're headed next."

On the first day of the summit, Toby and Laura stood side by side on the stage, the hall buzzing with energy as attendees from across the globe filled the seats.

Laura stepped forward, her voice confident and clear. "Welcome to the inaugural Global Summit of the Ashton Foundation. Today, we gather not just to share ideas but to ignite change—to build bridges across borders and to create a future where healthcare is a right, not a privilege." The applause was thunderous, the crowd's enthusiasm palpable.

Toby followed, his tone steady but heartfelt. "We're here because we believe in the power of connection. Every story we hear, every idea we share—it's part of a tapestry that binds us together. And as we look to the future, we must ask ourselves: How can we weave these threads into something greater than we've ever imagined?"

The summit featured a diverse lineup of speakers, from medical innovators and global health leaders to grassroots activists and educators. Each session sparked lively discussions, with participants sharing insights, challenges, and success stories.

During one panel on sustainable healthcare, Toby shared his experience from the Nairobi hospital, emphasizing the importance of collaboration and adaptability.

"True innovation comes from listening," he said. "It's about working hand in hand with communities to create solutions that are as unique as they are impactful."

Laura, meanwhile, led a workshop on building partnerships, her expertise and vision inspiring attendees to think creatively about leveraging resources and forging connections.

On the final evening of the summit, as the attendees gathered for a closing reception, Toby and Laura stood together on a balcony overlooking the lake.

"This feels like a dream," Laura said softly, her eyes reflecting the shimmering water. "But it's real, Toby. We did this."

Toby's smile was warm. "It's not just us. It's everyone who believed in this mission—everyone who took a step toward something bigger than themselves."

They clinked their glasses in a quiet toast, the moment a testament to their journey and the impact they continued to make.

As the summit ended, Toby and Laura knew it was just the beginning. The connections forged, the ideas shared, and the momentum generated promised to propel their foundation into a new era of global impact.

And as they said their goodbyes to the attendees, their hearts were full—not just with pride, but with hope for the future they were building together.

56

A Budding Dreamer

———◆◇◆———

It had always been clear to Toby and Laura that Liam carried a curiosity about the world around him. Whether he was building towers out of blocks or asking questions about the stars, his imagination seemed boundless, filled with the promise of new discoveries.

But as Liam grew, his questions began to touch on the work his parents were so passionate about—the trips they took, the people they helped, and the stories they shared.

One summer afternoon, Laura decided it was time to show Liam what their foundation was all about. She and Toby took him to one of their community clinics in Macon, a vibrant hub of activity where patients and healthcare providers bustled about with purpose.

As they entered the clinic, Liam's eyes widened with wonder. He clutched Toby's hand tightly, his curiosity evident as he took in the rows of chairs, the whirring machines, and the people who smiled warmly at him.

"This is where we help people," Laura explained gently, crouching down to meet Liam's gaze.

"Everyone here is working together to make sure people feel better and stay healthy." Liam nodded thoughtfully, his wide eyes taking in every detail.

During the visit, Liam observed Toby as he spoke with one of the clinic's nurses, explaining a new technique for managing patients with heart conditions. The nurse's admiration was clear, her respect for Toby's expertise shining through.

Liam tugged at Laura's hand, his voice soft but curious. "Is Daddy teaching her how to be a doctor?"

Laura smiled, her heart full. "He's sharing what he knows so that she can help even more people. That's what good doctors do—they take care of others and teach so everyone can grow."

Later, as they walked through the clinic, Liam met a young boy named Jacob, who was waiting for his appointment with his father. They quickly struck up a conversation about their favorite toys, their laughter filling the room.

"He's like me," Liam remarked as they left, his voice tinged with wonder. "But he doesn't feel good. Is he going to be okay?"

Toby leaned down, his tone steady and reassuring. "He's getting the help he needs. And you made him smile today—that's one of the best things you can do for someone."

That evening, as the family sat together on the porch, Liam looked up at the stars and began asking questions.

"Do people get better everywhere?" he asked, his voice tinged with both curiosity and concern.

Laura's smile was gentle. "Not everywhere yet, Liam. But that's what Mommy and Daddy are working on—making sure people everywhere have the help they need."

Liam's brow furrowed in thought. "I want to do that someday. I want to help people like you do."

Toby's heart swelled with pride as he met Liam's gaze. "You can do anything you dream of Liam. And we'll be here to help you every step of the way."

As Liam drifted off to sleep that night, his imagination alive with possibilities, Toby and Laura shared a quiet moment of reflection.

"He's starting to understand," Laura said softly. "What we do, why we do it—and that he can be part of it too."

Toby's smile was warm, his voice steady. "And whatever his dreams become, we'll make sure he knows he's capable of achieving them."

In Liam's budding curiosity, Toby and Laura saw not just the innocence of childhood but the promise of a future where compassion and hope could spark endless possibilities.

57

Weathering the Storm

———◆◇◆———

L ife had a way of throwing unexpected challenges even when everything seemed perfectly in place. Toby and Laura had spent years building their foundation, their family, and their connection to the communities they served. But one phone call on an ordinary Wednesday morning changed everything.

Laura answered the call while Toby played with Liam in the living room. Her expression shifted as she listened to the voice on the other end, her brow furrowing with worry.

"What do you mean the funding fell through?" Laura asked, her tone sharp but composed.

Toby turned to look at her, sensing the tension in her voice. Laura's conversation continued for several minutes before she hung up, her shoulders sagging under the weight of the news.

"We've lost the funding for one of the rural programs," she said softly, her voice tinged with disbelief. "It was a critical partnership, and now we're scrambling to keep it afloat."

Toby moved to her side, his gaze steady and supportive. "We'll figure this out, Laura. Let's sit down and go through our options."

The next several hours were spent brainstorming solutions, reaching out to contacts, and reviewing every detail of the program's budget. Despite their best efforts, the obstacles seemed insurmountable—the timing, the scope, and the sheer magnitude of the resources required.

"It feels like it's slipping away," Laura admitted late that evening, her voice breaking.

Toby wrapped his arms around her, his tone firm but kind. "You've built something incredible, Laura. And no matter what happens, we'll find a way forward—together."

As the days unfolded, their family became a source of comfort and inspiration. Robbie offered to help reach out to local business leaders for support, while Laura's parents shared ideas for organizing fundraising events.

Even Liam, in his childlike innocence, brought moments of lightness to their heavy hearts.

"Can I help, too?" Liam asked one afternoon, his wide eyes filled with sincerity.

"You already are," Laura replied, her smile soft as she hugged him. "Just by being you."

During one late-night meeting with Angela, an idea began to take shape—a grassroots campaign to raise awareness and secure small donations from individuals who believed in their mission.

"It's ambitious," Angela said, her tone thoughtful. "But if we can mobilize enough people, we might be able to bridge the gap."

The campaign launched within days, fueled by social media posts, heartfelt testimonials, and a series of community events. The response was overwhelming, with people from all levels of society contributing what they could to keep the program alive.

On the evening the campaign reached its fundraising goal, Toby and Laura sat on the porch, the glow of the sunset reflecting their quiet relief.

"We did it," Laura said softly, her voice filled with gratitude.

Toby's smile was warm. "No, Laura—you did it. You turned a setback into an opportunity—and you showed everyone what resilience really looks like."

Laura's eyes glistened with emotion as she leaned into him, their bond strengthened by the storm they had weathered together.

Though the crisis had tested them in ways they hadn't expected, it also reminded them of their strength—both as individuals and as partners. And as they looked to the future, they carried with them the belief that even the toughest challenges could spark something extraordinary.

58

An Unexpected Reunion

———◆◇◆———

It happened during a routine hospital visit—one of those days where Toby was balancing his time between mentoring residents, reviewing patient charts, and navigating the whirlwind of his growing responsibilities. As he walked through the lobby, he noticed a man standing by the reception desk, his profile vaguely familiar.

"Excuse me," the man said to the receptionist, his tone polite but tinged with uncertainty. "I'm looking for Dr. Ashton. I've been told he might be here today."

Toby's steps slowed, his mind racing to place the voice and the face. And then it hit him: Jason Miller, his old roommate from the Industrial Home.

"Jason?" Toby said softly, his voice carrying equal parts surprise and nostalgia.

Jason turned, his eyes widening as recognition crossed his face. "Toby? I can't believe it—it's really you!"

The embrace that followed was spontaneous and heartfelt, years of shared history bubbling to the surface as they exchanged hurried greetings.

"You've done well for yourself, Toby," Jason said, his gaze taking in Toby's crisp lab coat and confident demeanor. "I always knew you would."

Toby's smile was warm. "You've got to tell me what brought you here, Jason. I'd love to catch up."

Over coffee in the hospital's lounge, Jason began to share his journey—how he'd left the Industrial Home and built a career as a youth counselor, working tirelessly to support kids who reminded him of their younger selves.

"I always remembered the way you kept pushing forward," Jason said, his tone reflective. "It gave me hope, knowing that even the hardest circumstances couldn't stop us from chasing something better."

Toby listened intently, his respect for Jason's resilience growing with every word.

"And now you're saving lives, Toby," Jason continued, his voice tinged with admiration. "It's incredible, what you've achieved—and how you've stayed true to yourself."

Their conversation shifted to memories of the Industrial Home—the challenges they faced, the quiet moments of camaraderie, and the people who had shaped their paths.

"Do you ever think about Reverend Tanner?" Jason asked suddenly.

Toby's smile softened. "I do. He was one of the first people who believed in me—and he reminded me that even in the darkest times, there's always hope."

Jason nodded, his expression thoughtful. "I guess that's what we've carried with us all this time—the belief that we can make things better, no matter what."

As their conversation wound down, Jason shared an idea that had been lingering in his mind—a potential collaboration between Toby's foundation and the youth programs Jason had built.

"Kids like us—they need role models and mentors," Jason said, his tone earnest. "And I think the work you're doing could inspire them in ways we haven't even imagined."

Toby's heart swelled with excitement. "Let's make it happen, Jason. You've got my full support— and I know Laura will love the idea too."

As Jason prepared to leave, Toby felt a deep sense of gratitude for the unexpected reunion. Their shared history was a reminder of how far they had come—and of the bonds that had carried them forward.

"Don't be a stranger," Toby said as they parted ways. "We've got a lot to build together."

Jason's smile was bright. "Count on it, Toby. It's good to know some things don't change."

Later that evening, as Toby recounted the day to Laura on their porch, he found himself reflecting on the power of connection—the people who shaped us, the memories that ground us, and the friendships that remind us why we keep moving forward.

59

Robbie's Turn

———◦———

Robbie had always been the steady rock in Toby's life—the brother who had stood by him through every storm, offering humor and unwavering support when Toby needed it most. But as the family gathered at Mama's house for dinner one evening, Toby noticed something different about Robbie—an energy in his voice, a spark in his eyes that hinted at something stirring within.

As the laughter and clatter of dishes filled the room, Robbie cleared his throat, catching everyone's attention.

"I've got some news," he said, his voice tinged with both excitement and nervousness. "I've decided to take a big step—I'm opening my own carpentry business."

The room erupted into applause and cheers, the family's pride and support washing over Robbie like a warm wave.

"I've been thinking about this for a long time," Robbie continued, his smile wide. "I love what I do, and I want to turn it into something that's mine—something that can grow."

Toby stood and embraced his brother; his voice filled with encouragement. "You've got the talent, Robbie—and the heart. I know this is going to be amazing."

Over the next few weeks, Robbie poured himself into the process of starting his business— designing a logo, building a website, and setting up a workshop in town. Toby and Laura offered their support, helping him navigate the administrative side of entrepreneurship.

One afternoon, Robbie invited Toby to the workshop to show him a project he'd been working on—a beautifully crafted dining table made from reclaimed wood.

"This is incredible, Robbie," Toby said, running his hand over the smooth surface. "Every piece you make is going to tell a story."

Robbie's grin was wide. "That's the goal. I want people to feel like they're getting more than furniture—I want them to feel a connection."

As Robbie's business began to take off, he found himself spending time with someone new—a local artist named Grace who shared his passion for creativity and community.

"She's amazing," Robbie confided to Toby one evening. "She gets me in a way I didn't think was possible."

Toby's smile was warm. "You deserve someone who sees how incredible you are, Robbie. I can't wait to meet her."

Grace quickly became part of the family, her kindness and vibrant energy blending seamlessly with the close-knit group.

The journey wasn't without its hurdles. A delay in receiving materials for a large project left Robbie scrambling to meet a deadline, testing his patience and resolve.

"It's tough right now," Robbie admitted during a call with Toby. "But I'm learning as I go—and I think that's part of what makes this worth it."

Toby's voice was steady with reassurance. "You've always been the guy who figures it out, Robbie. You'll get through this—and you'll come out stronger."

Months later, the family gathered at Robbie's workshop to celebrate his first year in business. The space was filled with laughter, admiration for his work, and a deep sense of pride for how far he had come.

"You've built something incredible here," Toby said during a toast. "And it's not just the furniture—it's the way you've poured your heart into every step of this journey."

Robbie's smile was bright, his gratitude evident. "I couldn't have done it without all of you. This family—it's what keeps me going."

As Robbie's business continued to thrive, he found himself dreaming of new possibilities— expanding his workshop, collaborating with Grace on community projects, and building a future that was uniquely his own.

And as Toby watched his brother embrace this new chapter with courage and determination, he felt an overwhelming sense of pride—knowing that Robbie's strength, heart, and resilience were shaping a legacy all his own.

60

A New Chapter for Mama

The signs had been subtle at first—a forgotten conversation, misplaced keys, moments of confusion that Mama brushed off with a laugh and a wave of her hand. But during their visit home, Toby noticed something that made his heart sink: the flicker of uncertainty in her eyes as she struggled to recall the name of Liam's favorite toy.

It was Robbie who gently shared the news later that evening, pulling Toby aside as the rest of the family laughed and talked around the dinner table.

"She's been seeing a doctor," Robbie said softly, his voice steady but tinged with worry. "They've diagnosed her with Alzheimer's, Toby. She's doing okay for now, but... things are changing."

Toby felt the weight of Robbie's words settle over him like a heavy blanket. He glanced toward Mama, who was folding napkins with a practiced smile, completely unaware of their conversation.

"How long have you known?" Toby asked, his voice barely above a whisper.

"A few months," Robbie admitted. "I wanted to be sure before telling you—and to make sure we had a plan. We've found a facility nearby, one that specializes in memory care. She'll be safe there, and I'll visit her every day to make sure she's doing okay."

Toby nodded, his emotions a mix of gratitude for Robbie's strength and a deep ache at the thought of his mama moving away from the home that had been their anchor for so many years.

That evening, Toby sat with Mama on the porch, the quiet hum of crickets filling the air as the stars twinkled overhead.

"Mama," he said softly, his voice steady but filled with emotion. "Robbie told me about the diagnosis."

Mama's smile faltered for a moment before she reached for his hand, her touch gentle and reassuring.

"I've lived a good life, Toby," she said, her tone warm but firm. "And I'm not afraid of what's coming. What matters most to me is knowing that you boys and your families are happy—and that you'll carry everything I've taught you forward."

Toby swallowed hard, his voice breaking as he replied. "You've given us everything, Mama. And we'll be here for you, every step of the way."

In the days that followed, the family came together to prepare for the transition, each member contributing in their own way. Robbie organized the planning of the move, Laura worked with Toby to create a memory book filled with photos and stories to comfort Mama, and Liam spent hours drawing pictures to brighten her new room.

On the day of the move, Toby helped Mama settle into her new space, arranging the furniture and hanging the memory book where she could easily see it.

"This feels like home," Mama said with a smile as she traced her fingers over Liam's drawings. "You've made it beautiful."

Later, as Toby and Robbie stood together outside the facility, Toby turned to his brother, his voice steady but emotional.

"I'll come back as often as I can," Toby said. "I won't let her feel alone."

Robbie nodded, his gaze steady. "I'll keep a check on her, Toby—every day. She's well cared for, and we'll make sure she knows how much she's loved."

Toby's heart swelled with gratitude, his bond with Robbie strengthened by the shared promise to care for Mama in the days ahead.

As Toby drove back to the cottage with Laura and Liam, his emotions lingered in the quiet moments of the journey—gratitude for his family, hope for Mama's comfort, and the enduring love that carried them through even the most challenging times.

61

Full Circle

———◆◇◆———

It was during one of Laura's quiet evening reflections that the idea took shape. Sitting on the porch with Toby, the sounds of a distant cricket symphony wrapping around them, she turned to him, her voice filled with a quiet determination.

"We've done so much out there, Toby," she said. "But I keep thinking about where it all started—Pitney. There are still so many families there who need access to care."

Toby's gaze softened, his love for Laura's thoughtfulness evident. "I've been thinking the same thing. It's time we bring the foundation home."

The following week, Toby and Laura began planning an initiative to establish a state-of-the-art healthcare and education center in Pitney. It would provide medical services, wellness programs, and community workshops, all free of charge to the residents who had shaped their earliest years.

Their vision was bold: a place where people could feel supported and empowered, where young students could dream of careers in medicine, and where neighbors could build a healthier future together.

During a meeting with the foundation's leadership team, Laura outlined the plan. "This isn't just about healthcare," she explained. "It's about hope—about showing the people of Pitney that they're not forgotten."

As word of the initiative spread, the excitement was palpable. Toby and Laura hosted town halls to gather input from residents, ensuring the center reflected the unique needs and values of the community.

One evening, Mama joined them at a town hall, her presence a comforting reminder of the roots that grounded their mission.

"I'm so proud of you both," Mama said afterward, her voice soft but steady. "You're taking everything this town gave you and giving it back tenfold."

Robbie, too, offered his support, helping to design furniture for the center's waiting rooms. "This place is going to have heart," he said with a grin. "And not just because of the medical stuff."

The groundbreaking ceremony was a celebration of community spirit, with residents young and old gathering to mark the start of something extraordinary. Toby and Laura stood side by side, shovels in hand, as they turned the first pieces of earth.

"This isn't just our project," Toby said, addressing the crowd. "It's yours. Together, we're building a place that will bring comfort, care, and possibility to everyone who calls Pitney home." The applause that followed was thunderous, filled with hope and pride.

As construction progressed, Toby and Laura spent countless hours at the site, ensuring every detail reflected their vision. Laura collaborated with local artists to create murals that celebrated Pitney's history, while Toby worked with the medical team to design spaces that fostered both healing and connection.

One afternoon, as Liam played with a group of children near the construction site, Toby found himself reflecting on the significance of the project.

"This place—it's more than a building," he said to Laura. "It's a symbol of everything we believe in."

Months later, the Pitney Healthcare and Education Center opened its doors, a vibrant hub of activity and hope. The first day brought patients, families, and students eager to explore the services and opportunities the center offered.

Standing in the main lobby, surrounded by laughter and conversation, Toby and Laura felt an overwhelming sense of fulfillment.

"This is what it's all about," Laura said, her voice filled with pride. "Making a difference—right here, where it all began."

As the center flourished, Toby and Laura knew they had created something that would endure— a legacy rooted in love, resilience, and the belief that every community, no matter how small, deserved access to care and opportunity.

And as they walked through the halls, greeting neighbors, friends, and fresh faces alike, they felt the truth of what they had built together: a place where dreams could grow, where lives could be changed, and where the threads of their own story were forever woven into the fabric of Pitney.

62

Guiding the Next Generation

Toby had always believed that mentorship was a cornerstone of progress—a way to bridge gaps, foster growth, and pass on the knowledge and values that defined a profession. And after years of working with students, young doctors, and community health workers, he realized it was time to take mentorship to the next level.

Laura shared his enthusiasm; her voice filled with passion as they discussed the idea over dinner one evening.

"This program could be incredible, Toby," she said. "Imagine connecting students with professionals who not only teach them skills but inspire them to see healthcare as a way to transform lives."

Toby's smile was warm. "It's about shaping the next generation, Laura—giving them the tools and guidance to carry this mission forward long after we're gone."

The mentorship program—dubbed the Ashton Fellowship—was designed to pair aspiring healthcare professionals with experienced mentors from Toby and Laura's foundation and beyond.

The program aimed to provide more than just career guidance; it would focus on personal growth, community engagement, and the human connection at the heart of healthcare.

"You're not just training to be doctors or nurses," Toby explained during one of the first fellowship orientations. "You're training to be leaders, innovators, and compassionate caretakers. And through this program, you'll learn how to approach your work with heart and vision."

Toby and Laura reached out to their network of colleagues, friends, and allies to recruit mentors who embodied the program's values. From seasoned surgeons to community health advocates, the mentors brought a wealth of experience and a genuine desire to empower the next generation.

Dr. Evelyn Carter, one of Toby's former mentees, eagerly volunteered to join the program. "This is my chance to give back," she said. "To pass on what I've learned and to inspire students to think creatively and compassionately."

The program began with a series of workshops and networking events, where mentors and fellows were introduced and encouraged to share their stories and aspirations.

During one event, Toby noticed a young woman named Maya nervously approaching Dr. Carter. He watched as Maya's confidence grew with each word of encouragement from her mentor.

"You're exactly the kind of person this field needs, Maya," Carter said warmly. "And I'm here to help you see that every step of the way."

The exchange reminded Toby of his own journey—the mentors who had believed in him and the bonds that had carried him through his toughest challenges.

As the Siler Fellowship gained momentum, its impact began to ripple out into the communities the fellows served. The program's graduates returned to their hometowns with renewed energy, launching clinics, advocating for policy changes, and mentoring others in turn.

During a reunion event, one fellow shared a story of how their mentor had shaped their career. "Dr. Ashton taught me to never lose sight of the human connection," they said. "It's what drives everything we do—and it's what keeps us grounded."

As Toby and Laura reflected on the success of the program, they felt a deep sense of fulfillment—not just for the lives they were touching today but for the legacy they were building for the future.

"It's incredible to see how far they've come," Laura said as they watched a group of fellows presenting their ideas at a symposium. "And it's even more incredible to think about how far they'll go."

Toby nodded, his heart full. "This is what it's all about—guiding them to see not just what's possible but what's meaningful."

63

Growing Hearts, Growing Home

———◆◇◆———

The day had begun like any other—Liam chasing butterflies in the yard, Laura sipping her morning coffee on the porch, and Toby thumbing through patient notes before heading to the hospital. But as Laura stood in front of the bathroom mirror, holding the test that confirmed what she'd quietly suspected for weeks, she felt her world shift ever so slightly.

A new life was on its way, and with it, a flood of emotions—joy, hope, and a touch of nervous excitement.

That evening, Laura waited until Liam had fallen asleep before pulling Toby aside. As they sat together on the couch, she slipped the test into his hand, her smile filled with emotion.

Toby stared at it for a moment before his gaze met hers, his expression a mix of surprise and elation.

"Are you serious?" he asked softly, his voice catching.

Laura nodded, her eyes glistening. "We're going to have another baby, Toby. Our family is growing."

Toby's grin spread across his face as he pulled her into an embrace, his heart full. "I can't believe it. Laura, this is incredible."

The next morning, they sat Liam down at the breakfast table, their excitement tempered with care as they prepared to share the news.

"Liam," Toby began, his tone warm and gentle, "Mommy and Daddy have something special to tell you."

Liam looked up from his pancakes, his curiosity piqued. "What is it?"

Laura's smile widened. "You're going to be a big brother, sweetheart. There's a baby growing in Mommy's tummy."

Liam's eyes grew wide with wonder as he processed the news. "A baby? Like me?"

Toby chuckled, his love for Liam evident. "Just like you, buddy. And you're going to be the best big brother ever."

Liam's face broke into a grin as he clapped his hands. "I'm going to teach them everything—like how to draw and how to find the best rocks!"

When Laura and Toby shared the news with their extended family over dinner, the room erupted into cheers and laughter. Mama's eyes filled with tears of joy, while Robbie enveloped Laura in a bear hug.

"This family just keeps getting better and better," Robbie said with a grin.

Laura's parents, beaming with pride, began brainstorming ways to support the growing family— whether it was repainting the nursery or babysitting Liam during doctor's appointments.

"We're here for you, every step of the way," Laura's mom assured them, her voice steady with love.

As the weeks passed, Toby and Laura found themselves daydreaming about the future— decorating the nursery, imagining Liam playing with his sibling, and reflecting on the journey that had brought them to this moment.

One evening, as they sat together on the porch watching the fireflies dance in the twilight, Laura turned to Toby with a thoughtful expression.

"Do you ever feel like life is giving us more than we could have ever asked for?" she asked softly.

Toby reached for her hand, his gaze steady. "Every day, Laura. And I wouldn't trade a single moment of it."

With every passing day, the anticipation grew, filling their home with hope and love. Liam's excitement was contagious, his endless curiosity about the baby sparking laughter and warmth.

As they prepared for the arrival of their newest family member, Toby and Laura knew that their hearts—and their home—were ready to welcome this new chapter of joy, growth, and connection.

64

Expanding Horizons

---◆○◆---

The opportunities had been building for years, as word of Toby's innovative techniques in cardiology spread throughout the medical community. Invitations poured in from hospitals and medical schools across the country, each one eager to learn from the groundbreaking work Toby had pioneered.

After much discussion with Laura and the foundation's leadership team, Toby decided it was time to take his expertise on the road, traveling to train physicians and share his knowledge.

"This is your chance to multiply the impact," Laura said one evening as they finalized his itinerary. "Every doctor you train will go on to help countless patients—and that's a legacy worth building."

Toby's travels took him to cities large and small, from bustling urban centers to rural hospitals where resources were scarce but the determination to provide care was immense.

At each stop, Toby led workshops, hands-on demonstrations, and lectures that focused on minimally invasive techniques, patient-centered care, and the art of balancing precision with compassion.

One morning, at a teaching hospital in Chicago, a young resident approached him after a session. "Dr. Ashton, your work is inspiring," she said. "It's changed the way I think about medicine—and about the kind of doctor I want to be."

Toby's smile was warm as he replied, "It's not just about the techniques. It's about seeing the patient behind the diagnosis—and never losing sight of why we do what we do."

Back in Pitney, Laura took charge of maintaining their clinic, her steady presence and leadership ensuring that the community continued to receive the care they needed.

Under her guidance, the clinic thrived, with innovative programs launched to support maternal health, chronic disease management, and mental wellness. Laura's passion for connecting with patients and staff alike created an atmosphere of trust and hope.

During one staff meeting, Angela remarked, "Laura, you make everyone here feel like family— and that's what makes this clinic so special."

Laura smiled, her heart full. "It's because we are a family—every patient, every staff member, and every person who walks through these doors."

Despite Toby's demanding travel schedule, he, and Laura made it a priority to stay connected, sharing nightly phone calls and planning regular weekends at home to spend time with Liam and prepare for their growing family.

One evening, after finishing a workshop in Seattle, Toby Face-Timed Laura and Liam, his heart lifting at the sight of their smiling faces.

"Guess what, Daddy?" Liam said excitedly. "I helped Mommy water the plants at the clinic today!"

Toby chuckled, his love for his family shining through. "That's my boy—already making a difference."

Toby's travels not only strengthened his reputation as a leader in cardiology but also deepened his understanding of the challenges faced by physicians in diverse settings.

At a rural hospital in New Mexico, he worked closely with a group of doctors to adapt his techniques to their limited resources, emphasizing the importance of creativity and teamwork.

"These techniques are just tools," Toby explained during one session. "It's your dedication and innovation that turn them into life-saving solutions."

As Toby returned home after months on the road, he and Laura reflected on the impact of their work—the lives they touched, the connections they built, and the dreams they continued to chase.

"We're on this journey together," Toby said one evening as they sat on the porch, the glow of the setting sun painting the sky in hues of orange and gold.

Laura reached for his hand, her gaze steady. "And every step we take brings us closer to the world we're working to create—a world where everyone has access to care, compassion, and hope."

65

A Beacon of Excellence

———◄○►———

The Pitney Healthcare and Education Center had always been envisioned as a place of hope—a haven for care, learning, and connection. But what began as a heartfelt dream soon grew into something far greater, as word of the center's innovative programs spread across the nation.

Within just a few years, the center became one of the most sought-after training facilities for healthcare professionals, drawing physicians, nurses, and medical students from every corner of the country to the small town of Pitney.

It started with a single article in a prestigious medical journal, highlighting the center's unique approach to mentorship and hands-on training. Shortly after, conferences and speaking engagements followed, and soon, Pitney was bustling with visitors eager to learn from the facility's groundbreaking methods.

"This place is changing the way medicine is taught and practiced," said Dr. Patel, one of Toby's mentors, during a visit to the center. "And it's putting Pitney on the map in a way no one could have imagined."

Toby's gratitude was evident as he replied, "It's all thanks to the incredible team we've built— and the heart of this community."

The influx of physicians and medical professionals brought a wave of economic growth to Pitney, revitalizing the town with new businesses, restaurants, and housing developments.

Laura and Toby watched with awe as the streets they had known since childhood transformed into hubs of activity, filled with energy and possibility.

"It feels surreal," Laura remarked one afternoon as they strolled through downtown, passing families, students, and professionals who had come to be part of the center's legacy. "This town—it's alive in a way I've never seen before."

Toby nodded, his pride evident. "And it's all because people believed in what we were building—and what this community could become."

The center's training programs grew to include simulations, case-based learning, and partnerships with medical schools nationwide. Physicians who had trained at the center carried their knowledge and passion back to their hometowns, creating a ripple effect of innovation and care.

During one training session, Toby overheard a young doctor from Minnesota sharing her gratitude.

"Coming here has changed the way I see medicine," she said. "This isn't just about saving lives— it's about connecting with people, inspiring hope, and creating change."

Pitney flourished with the opportunities the center brought. Old buildings were revitalized into research labs, coffee shops, and learning spaces. The once-sleepy town became a vibrant hub for professionals and families alike, attracting attention and admiration from across the country.

Residents who had lived in Pitney for generations felt a renewed sense of pride, knowing that their small town had become a beacon of excellence and compassion.

One evening, as Toby and Laura sat together on the porch overlooking the bustling streets of Pitney, they found themselves reflecting on the journey that had brought them here.

"It's hard to believe how much has changed," Toby said softly.

Laura's smile was steady. "And yet, the heart of this town—the people who made it what it is— that's stayed the same."

Toby reached for her hand, his love for her and for Pitney evident. "We've built something incredible here, Laura. And the best part is knowing that this is just the beginning."

As the center continued to thrive, Toby and Laura carried with them the knowledge that their vision had transformed not just lives but an entire community. And as they looked to the horizon, they knew that the threads they had woven into Pitney's tapestry would endure for generations to come.

Epilogue

THE TAPESTRY OF THEIR LIVES

The sun hung low on the horizon, casting warm hues of amber and gold over the rolling hills that framed their backyard. Toby sat on the old wooden porch swing, its familiar creak blending into the symphony of chirping crickets and rustling leaves. A gentle breeze carried the sweet scent of wildflowers from the garden Laura had tended to so lovingly over the years.

He closed his eyes for a moment, letting the memories come. The faces, the voices, the countless hands he'd held over the decades—they were all stitched into the fabric of his life, a vibrant tapestry of hope, resilience, and connection.

Toby thought of the patients who had entrusted their lives to him, the students who had carried his lessons into the world, and the colleagues who had pushed boundaries alongside him. He thought of the town of Pitney—once quiet and unassuming, now bustling with energy and pride—a community transformed by the dreams he and Laura had dared to pursue.

His gaze shifted to the far edge of the yard, where Liam had once played with his little sister under the shade of the oak tree. They were grown now, each chasing dreams of their own. Liam, a teacher with a passion for shaping young minds, and his sister, a physician carrying on the legacy of care and compassion she'd witnessed growing up.

"They've become everything we hoped for," Toby said softly, his voice breaking the quiet.

Laura, who had been watering the lavender at the edge of the porch, joined him on the swing, her presence as comforting as it had been on the very first day they'd met. She leaned into him, resting her head on his shoulder, and together they watched the sun dip lower in the sky.

"They've found their way, Toby," Laura replied, her voice warm and steady. "And so have we."

Toby turned to look at her, his heart full. "Do you ever think about where it all began? That first clinic, the porch conversations, the long nights when we weren't sure if any of it would work?"

Laura's smile was wistful. "I think about it all the time. Every struggle, every triumph—it's all brought us here. And I wouldn't change a single moment."

Toby's thoughts wandered to the countless lives they'd touched—not just the patients who had walked through their doors, but the young doctors and nurses who had found inspiration in their mentorship, the communities they'd lifted, and the friends they'd made along the way.

"It's funny," Toby said, his tone reflective. "When you're in the thick of it, you don't always realize the impact you're having. But looking back... I see it now. The lives we've been a part of—they're part of us too."

Laura reached for his hand, her fingers intertwining with his. "That's the beauty of it, Toby. It's all connected—the people who shaped us, the people we've helped, the love and hope that keep us moving forward. It's a legacy that doesn't end with us."

They sat in silence for a while, the twilight settling around them like a warm embrace. The stars began to emerge one by one, tiny pinpricks of light that stretched endlessly across the sky.

"This is enough, isn't it?" Toby said softly, his voice filled with a quiet contentment. "The work we've done, the family we've built, the memories we've made—it's more than I could have ever dreamed."

Laura smiled, her eyes shimmering in the starlight. "It's more than enough, Toby. It's everything."

As the night deepened, they stayed there on the swing, side by side, the echoes of their journey lingering in the air. The world around them may have changed, but here, in this quiet moment, they were simply Toby and Laura—the boy from Pitney who never stopped dreaming and the woman who stood by his side through it all.

Their story, though written in the stars and carried in the hearts of those they'd touched, remained theirs. And as the gentle hum of the night enveloped them, they knew that their legacy of love, compassion, and hope would live on—woven into the lives of generations to come.

Other Books by Dr. Cravey may be found on Amazon.com or http://drcharlescravey.com

www.ingramcontent.com/pod-product-compliance
Lightning Source LLC
Chambersburg PA
CBHW060348030726
47497CB00003B/638